The Bad Samaritan
The Masters of the House
A Hovering of Vultures
A Fatal Attachment
A Scandal in Belgravia
A City of Strangers
Death of a Salesperson
Death and the Chaste Apprentice
At Death's Door
The Skeleton in the Grass
The Cherry Blossom Corpse
Bodies
Political Suicide
Fete Fatale
Out of the Blackout
Corpse in a Gilded Cage
School for Murder
The Case of the Missing Bronte
A Little Local Murder
Death and the Princess
Death by Sheer Torture
Death in a Cold Climate
Death of a Perfect Mother
Death of a Literary Widow
Death of a Mystery Writer
Blood Brotherhood
Death on the High C's
Death of an Old Goat

ROBERT BARNARD

The Habit of Widowhood

SCRIBNER

SCRIBNER
1230 Avenue of the Americas
New York, NY 10020

1996 Robert Barnard—collection and introduction
Robert Barnard 1990, 1991, 1989, 1992, 1993, 1994, 1986, 1995, 1987, 1988

The following stories first appeared in the U.S. in *Ellery Queen's Mystery Magazine:* "Cupid's Dart"; "The Habit of Widowhood"; "Post Mortem"; "Soldier, from the Wars Returning"; "My Son, My Son"; "The Stuff of Nightmares"; "Balmorality"; "Living with Jimmy"; "If Looks Could Kill"; "Reader, I Strangled Him"; "The Gentleman in the Lake"; "The Women at the Funeral"; "Perfect Honeymoon"; and "More Final Than Divorce"; "Happy Christmas" appeared in *Ellery Queen's Prime Crimes 4,* and "Dog Television" in *Malice Domestic 11.* "Called to Judgment" is here published for the first time.

SCRIBNER and design are registered trademarks of Simon & Schuster Inc.

Designed by Jenny Dossin
Text set in Adobe Caslon

Manufactured in the United States of America

1 3 5 7 9 10 8 6 4 2

Library of Congress Cataloging-in-Publication Data
Barnard, Robert.
The habit of widowhood/Robert Barnard.
p. cm.
1. Detective and mystery stories, English. I. Title
PR6052.A665H33 1996
623'.914—dc20 96-6952 CIP

ISBN 0-684-82648-8

CONTENTS

D92889

The Habit of Widowhood

INTRODUCTION

It is difficult to imagine today the excited anticipation with which the turn-of-the-century reader awaited the next exploit of Sherlock Holmes in the *Strand* magazine or (more, because a criminal hero was rather shocking) the next felonious enterprise of Raffles and Bunny. Nowadays, outside of the wonderful *Ellery Queen's Mystery Magazine,* the crime short story gets published only occasionally in newspaper supplements and glossy monthlies. The formula of the character or the duo who run through a series of adventures or feats of detection is used by hardly anyone—though what a good formula it is!

And what opportunities the short story offers to the writer who is willing to learn to operate within its disciplines. It is, first of all, a medium in which every word has to be made to tell: a paragraph in a short story equals, sweat-wise, three or four pages in a straightforward crime novel. Economy is the watchword, and it involves weighting every word so that it will have maximum impact or carry the greatest number of possible implications. It is the opposite of the word-processing writer's disease: burbling on about nothing very much because it's so easy.

Lacking the wider canvas of the full-length crime novel—especially nowadays, when "full-length" is very long indeed—the short story is closer to a snapshot than to a movie. The significant moment is explored in depth, the single relationship or predicament is illumined, the crisis highlighted that will lead to violence. Because the crime short story these days is seldom a whodunit, the writer can go in depth into sad or horrible lives without fear that he is "giving away" a solution. And, perhaps above all, he can change tone from the ironic to the terrifying, with a hundred nice gradations in between, and he can choose the kind of story he wants to write, from the humorous send-up to the serious exploration of the criminal mind. Once you have accustomed yourself to the tiny canvas the number of different effects you can achieve with the small brush is amazing.

Tastes change. The sort of people who clamored for the latest Holmes story had different needs and lifestyles from the people a generation or two earlier who clamored for the latest number of a Dickens novel. Perhaps the people who get on the Underground or subway and open up their Jeffrey Archer or Barbara Taylor Bradford at the page they'd got to when they reached their destination the day before will some-day come to realize the greater variety of the short story, the wide range of stimuli it can encompass, the number of worlds it can open up. Let's hope so.

R. B.

CUPID'S DART

I smile sometimes when I read articles in the newspapers about arranged marriages in the Asian community. I read a lot now—well, I suppose I always did, but I read different things now: newspapers, magazines, things that tell me what life is like, what goes on in the world. So when I read about arranged marriages I smile, because the writers always seem so complacent: this is a strange, foreign custom, they seem to be saying, which is quite alien to our native, white tradition. Yet my marriage was arranged as surely as any Moslem girl's, and I went into it with as little knowledge of my husband-to-be.

Oh, I had seen him before. I gather from the articles that in some, extreme cases, the first a Moslem bride sees of the man is at the ceremony. In my case Mr. Hatfield had been to tea. I remember my mother telling me of this in advance: "We've invited Mr. Hatfield, from church, to come to tea." I remember feeling vaguely bewildered as to what inviting someone to tea entailed. Was it a verb or a noun, how was it spelt? I was eighteen at the time.

I sometimes wonder how it came about that I slipped so entirely through what the newspapers call "the welfare net." And it wasn't simply the social workers who were unaware of my existence: school inspectors, the local government bureaucracy, the national bureaucracy, all—it emerged later—were quite unaware that at 41 Wilton Grange Avenue there was living not only Mr. and Mrs. William Derbyshire, but also a daughter, Jessica. Certainly no neighbor ever felt worried enough about me to contact the authorities, but then, this was London, where neighbors keep themselves to themselves. And what was there to be worried about?

I think the reason for my nonappearance on registers and lists, voting rolls and official records, was partly my parents' reluctance that I should, partly the circumstances of my birth. I was born on the island of Madagascar, where my father (who was over forty at the time of my birth, as was my mother) held some sort of official diplomatic post—I think he was British Vice-Consul or something of the kind. He was not an effectual man, not one likely to be a success in any job requiring decision-making or organizational skills. I think he disliked the place, and that the sun got to him ("Sit in the *shade*, dear, it's much safer," my mother always used to say to me on summer days). Anyway, it seems he became slightly odd, and was retired with a pension in 1969, when I was eighteen months old. So they returned home by cargo ship, and bought a house in Wilton Grange Avenue, and if they never consciously decided to keep my existence a secret, and I really don't think they did, then they certainly never advertised it to officialdom either.

I think coming home to Britain at the height of the permissive revolution (something I knew nothing about at the time, of course, though I've read a great deal about it recently) strengthened the feelings they already had about the world. Here was a strange land of miniskirts and pot, of flagrantly explicit pop lyrics and men saying "fuck" on television. (It is a word I cannot say, only write, even now.) I think they saw Britain from the start as a place of corruption. This went hand in hand with various other oddities, or what would have seemed like oddities to people at the time: a drab, evangelical religion, a preference for homeopathic medicine (I was on no doctor's register throughout my childhood), a refusal to own a television or take a newspaper. Not criminal, any of these things, or even outrageously odd—but they added up to a rejection of the world around them. So did their failure to send me to any kind of school, or to procure me any sort of companionship of children of my own age. There was them and me, in the house, alone.

I was, as they used to say about genteel girls long ago, "educated privately at home." They must have taught me to read, and to add up and subtract. Then they just let me loose on the faded, musty collection of books that was dotted around the house: *Peter Pan, The Wind in the Willows, Five Go Adventuring Again.* There were elementary books about flowers and plants, religious books with pictures of a brown-bearded Christ, there was a globe, and a wall poster of the monarchs of England from 1066 to George V (it had been printed, of course, in their childhood). If I showed any curiosity about anything they answered my questions. If the question was historical, their answers would have the flavor of a late-Victorian history book: Queen Elizabeth rallying the troops at Tilbury, the Battle of Waterloo being won on the playing fields of Eton—that kind of thing. If my questions were geographical, their answers would be flavored by a sort of controlled distaste for foreign countries that could not really be called chauvinism, since they exhibited the same sort of controlled distaste for Britain and the British.

So that was my childhood. We had a wireless, and sometimes we listened to it—the midmorning story, or *Your Hundred Best Tunes.* At moments of national crisis (elections, the Falklands war) we listened to the news, though I never remember my parents commenting on it afterwards. In the evenings we sometimes played draughts, or did an old jigsaw puzzle. In the garden, if it was fine, I might do some weeding or planting, or make friends with the neighbors' cat if I was shielded by a bush. We had no animal, because my father thought them inherently filthy and a source of disease: he got angry when a dog peed against our front gatepost, and the other thing he referred to as "feces" with an expression of distaste so strong as to be obsessional.

It was, I recognize now, an extremely boring childhood. I did not see it like that at the time, because I had been conditioned to boredom from my earliest years. If I read in an Enid Blyton story about children who got together and had fun and adventures, I knew that this would not happen to me and accepted the fact. I was different, and I had Mummy and Daddy, who protected me from harm and kissed me on my birthday.

When I left the house it was to go to church. Quite early in my childhood my parents began to go to the Congregation of the Divine Elect. This was a tiny group, meeting in what was not much more than a stone-dashed hut, which followed its own doctrines and made its own disciplines. It was nearly two miles away, and as we had no car and my parents disliked using public transport, we walked there on Sunday mornings, me in one of my much-washed print dresses, and when it was over we walked back again, through the streets of South London. I don't remember ever being told to keep my eyes on the pavement as I walked, but my parents did and so I did. But I did see out of the corners of my eyes hints of the world: dirty children playing and laughing, newspaper hoardings shrieking sensational stories I could barely understand, black people, people who took off their clothes in the summer sun, young people holding hands. They remained hints only, for on the whole I refrained from asking questions. I was not an incurious child, but I had learnt that my curiosity was never really satisfied by my parents.

I cannot say what the Congregation of the Divine Elect believed in. To their credit they did not believe that they *were* the divine elect, merely by the fact of their making their way to that ugly little box in the side street in Croydon. Nevertheless they were extremely interested in probing who *were* the elect, for, like most nonconformist sects, they did not regard it as presumptuous to scan the ways of God, and many of them over the years convinced themselves that they had got to know his likes and dislikes quite well. There was no regular minister, and a different member of the Congregation led the meeting (they preferred not to call it a "service") each week, interrupted by anyone who felt called upon to bear witness or testify—usually to some example of God's goodness to him, or punishment of him, or some revelation personally vouchsafed during the past week. We had just one hymn, from a meager, roneoed collection, and we went our ways soberly at the end. I can't say it meant much to me, but it made a change.

And so the years passed. I began reading different books— *Kidnapped, Berry and Co., Oliver Twist.* And as well as reading, I began to like music. I was allowed to listen to concerts on the wireless, though I think my parents got little pleasure from them themselves, and it was never suggested that I might learn an instrument. My body grew and there were strange changes in it which frightened me at first. But my mother merely said, shortly and dryly: "It's natural. It always happens." So I suppose I stopped being afraid.

I reached eighteen without being aware that there was anything special about being eighteen. If any coming-of-age was celebrated in any of the books in the house, it would have been a twenty-first. So I became legally adult and eligible to vote (except that I was on no electoral rolls) without anything being said about it. But my parents (who were now *old*, even I could see that) registered that time was passing. It was about three weeks after my birthday that my mother said, apparently casually:

"We've invited Mr. Hatfield, from church, to come to tea on Friday."

At the time I merely nodded, being uncertain, as I said, of what coming to tea implied, and not being sure either which of the Congregation's members Mr. Hatfield was. In the course of Friday I discovered what having someone to tea implied, for my mother's preparations, though modest, were undoubtedly special. She bought a small brown and a small white loaf, cut them more thinly than usual, and spread some with something called Sandwich Spread, some with salmon and shrimp paste, and some with an egg mayonnaise which she had concocted herself. She also brought out a jam sponge which had been bought at the local supermarket (I had never been myself to a supermarket, but my mother or my father always did the weekly shop there, I think because they liked the anonymity). This sponge she cut up early on, so that the edges of the slice I had at tea were already slightly crisp. All these preparations were done rather clumsily, as befitted a ceremonial meal that was thirty or forty years out of date. Everything was already set out, waiting only a fresh brew of tea, when Mr. Hatfield arrived.

He was a man in his fifties whom I had seen my parents exchanging the occasional word with after the Sunday meeting. He was stout, decidedly so, but he seemed well-meaning, and had a little goatee beard. The Congregation disapproved of display in dress (it was easier to say what the Congregation disapproved of than to say what they believed in), but for this tea Mr. Hatfield was besuited, undoubtedly tidy and spruce, and even sported a white carnation in his buttonhole.

Oddly enough what I remember about that occasion was our tea service, which I sat looking at much of the time. I compared this tea with great social occasions in books, and I saw that our tea service wasn't up to par: each cup and saucer suffered from small chips or cracks, and the colored pattern was dingy; only the slops basin, hardly ever used, had any freshness.

Mr. Hatfield talked mostly to my parents, and even with them things were not easy. My mother and father had few topics of conversation because they had few interests. Eventually when they got on to homeopathy things went more easily, my father having some expertise in that field. Occasionally Mr. Hatfield would address a remark to me.

"I hear you're fond of music."

"Yes, I am."

"I have a very old record player, but I've not acquired a great record collection, I'm afraid."

I nodded, not seeing the relevance of this. I wondered what time a coming to tea ended, because there was something I wanted to hear on the wireless that evening.

In another interval in the conversation he said:

"Do you enjoy cooking?"

That puzzled me rather. I didn't see how one could enjoy cooking, which in our household meant the provision of meals. However, I said, "Yes, I do quite enjoy cooking," in my clear, old-fashioned way, and that seemed to satisfy him.

He went at six, saying he had to attend a meeting of the Elders of the Congregation. I was pleased, because I wanted to listen to *Lucia di Lammermoor*, relayed from Covent Garden. I had very little idea what seeing an opera would be like, but I loved hearing them. I now knew what having someone to tea meant, and I put Mr. Hatfield from my mind.

Until, that is, five or six days later, when my mother came into the sitting room, where I was reading in the light of a rather dismal day.

"Jessica, your father and I have been giving a lot of thought to what is to happen to you after we are gone."

I knew that "gone" meant "dead" in my mother's language, and she rather frightened me.

"Can't I go on living here?"

"We don't see how. Your father's pension dies with us. You see, we have . . . we have had an offer of marriage for you—from Mr. Hatfield, at church."

I knew then and there that this was something that they had arranged themselves. I also knew that, in their way, their motives were well-meaning. I sat quiet for some moments, grateful for my book to look at.

"Marriage?" I said at last. "I don't really understand what that means."

"It means you would live with him as man and wife. Like Daddy and me." She added rather awkwardly: "Mr. Hatfield will show you what it means."

"I see," I said.

"Your father and I think you should accept. For your future."

I thought for a few moments more. Mr. Hatfield had seemed a fairly amiable man. Perhaps if I had been more used to choice I would have been better equipped to say no, but my life had had few alternatives, and fewer still where I had been the one who decided.

"All right," I said.

Oddly enough, I did not see Mr. Hatfield again in the days before the wedding. Presumably he did not think it worthwhile to get to know me better. I suspect he was spring-cleaning his house, which had doubtless been neglected in the years since his first wife died. The wedding was set for a fortnight after my mother's announcement to me (that was what I felt it amounted to). Toward the end of that time they packed my clothes and a few other personal things into two very old suitcases. These my father took round to Mr. Hatfield's house on the day before the wedding. I wondered how I would do without the books.

I married Mr. Hatfield, in fact, twice. The Congregation was not legally entitled to perform the sacrament of marriage, so we had to go through a Registry Office ceremony first. It was not much of a ceremony (but then neither was the Congregation's), but I did learn for the first time that my husband's Christian name was Felix. The Registry Office, a little off our route, was still only five minutes from the Congregation, and we walked on there—Mr. Hatfield, my parents, and me, me in one of the two or three faded print dresses I wore regularly to church. Mr. Hatfield wore the suit he had worn to tea with us, now with a brilliant red carnation in his buttonhole.

The Congregation had had a bit of trouble over their marriage service, or meeting as they called it, the last one having been over twelve years previously, and what they came up with did not have a great deal of shape to it. First there was a hymn—"For All the Saints." The Congregation sang remarkably badly for nonconformists. Then Mr. Potts was moved to share with us a feeling which he suggested was divinely inspired and which had come to him in the course of the week: this, I gathered, was that our union would be long, happy, and fruitful. Then the leader for that week led us in a rather bare version of the marriage service, in which I promised to love and honor Mr. Hatfield, and he promised to do the same by me. Then, thankfully, it was all over. There was tea afterward (there was a gas ring at the back of the church), and someone had brought along a supermarket cake. Everyone quietly wished us well. I don't remember any of them showing signs of embarrassment but I am not sure I would have recognized what embarrassment was.

Quite soon we went home—only of course it was a new "home." My parents walked with us for five minutes, but then we all stopped and it was indicated that Mr. Hatfield and I would now turn off. Both my parents kissed me, increasing my sense of this as a special day, and my mother told me to be a good girl. Then Mr. Hatfield and I continued on our way in the bustle of early evening, through strange streets that were yet very much like the streets I already knew. Mr. Hatfield made sober conversation. I already had a slight sense that there was a difference between the public Mr. Hatfield and the private one, though it was not something I could pin down in words. He said it had been a very moving service, that Mr. Potts had spoken most impressively, that the good wishes of the Congregation had been most gratifying. I said yes to all these propositions. Quite soon we arrived at 10 Mafeking Terrace, Mr. Hatfield's home.

You will perhaps not realize how strange it felt, going into this house. You see, I had never, in my memory, been in anyone's home other than my own. It was spotlessly clean, but the furniture was old and very shabby. Mr. Hatfield, I learned later, was a commercial traveler, and not well off. I saw my cases in the hall, and when we went through into the dining room I saw the table laid for two.

"Just a modest meal," said Mr. Hatfield, "something I can heat up in the oven." He smiled with a hint of roguishness. "An intimate meal for two."

He went over to a wooden box in the corner and pressed a

button. In a moment, astonishingly, a talking face appeared on a screen. This must be television, which I had heard about but never seen. I stood there in the middle of the room, looking, entranced.

"Just hear the news headlines."

I did not register what they were talking about, only that here was a handsome man and a pretty woman telling us things. After a minute or two Mr. Hatfield went to turn it off, but he saw me still transfixed by the pictures, and he took himself off to the kitchen. As I watched, things gradually began to make some sense: there was a war somewhere abroad, there was a football team playing another football team, there was the Queen (I recognized her) opening a bridge somewhere in the North of the country. All in enchanting pictures. It was as good as a book.

When it was over Mr. Hatfield turned it off. It became a box again. He said: "Perhaps you'd help me serve up dinner."

I went with him into the kitchen, which like the rest of the house was clean but shabby. The dinner certainly didn't need much serving up. It was in the oven in two silver dishes—each one holding the whole meal: roast beef, roast potatoes, carrots and peas, all in a rich brown gravy. I know because I read the cardboard container it had come in. I thought it was wonderful. We transferred it on to our plates, and carried it through to the dining room. "Soon you can cook me really nice meals," said Mr. Hatfield, smiling encouragingly. I did not see any point at all in all the preparation that cookery usually involved when you could get lovely meals like this. But I nodded—I nodded a lot that day.

While we ate, Mr. Hatfield made little dribbles of good-humored conversation, with sometimes the odd roguish joke which I did not then understand. But I think he saw my eyes straying sideways to the television box in the corner. I was wondering whether it was quiet because there was nothing on it or because he had switched it off. He saw my fascination (I realize now that he was a kindly man), and when we had eaten a sponge pudding with syrup over it, also from a cardboard container I had seen in the kitchen, he switched it on again.

This time it was even more wonderful. It was what I now know was a "soap": people in a street, quarreling, laughing, drinking, kissing. It was like suddenly seeing the world. I sat on the sofa, and when he had washed up the plates Mr. Hatfield sat beside me. He put his arm around my shoulders, and when the people on the box kissed he bent over and kissed me on the cheek—not on the lips as they did, because I did not turn my face away from the screen. After the people in the street there were American policemen, and then people playing some sort of game. It was wonderful, enthralling.

"I don't think your parents would approve," said Mr. Hatfield.

I did not know whether or not they would approve, but I did know they would not themselves have watched.

At half past nine Mr. Hatfield pressed the switch again.

"Time for beddy-byes," he said, with a funny wry smile and a spark in his eyes. I nodded. I went to bed around that time as a rule, and I presumed the television people must close down then.

I saw in the hall that the small suitcase with my night things and a change of clothes had gone. As we went up the stairs, Mr. Hatfield put his arm around my waist, which I did not like but did not know how to stop. In the bedroom the light was already on, and I saw that my nightdress had been laid out on an enormous bed. I waited for Mr. Hatfield to go, but he did not. He shut the door, and then came over and began fumbling with the buttons at the back of my dress.

"Don't," I said.

I did not know what to do. I couldn't tell him to go away in his own house. I took my nightdress and went over to a dark corner, where I removed my dress and petticoat as modestly as I could, then put my nightdress on and removed my other clothes. I knew that Mr. Hatfield had not gone away and I did not want to turn round, but in the end I did not know what else to do.

It was horrible. He had taken all his clothes off, and I saw that he was not made like me. As I watched, my heart beating fiercely, the thing beneath his fat belly began rising and growing big.

"Look! Cupid's dart!" he said, with a dreadful jollity. "I'm going to teach you all about it."

I don't know how I managed to endure it. Somehow I seemed to detach my mind so that I could relax. I must have seemed quite limp, dead, as he led me to the bed, pulled up my nightdress and began doing what he wanted to do to me. But if my mind was in another place it was also, or part of it, screaming with nausea and humiliation. He switched out the light from beside the bed, and I felt him on top of me, and part of me was howling with terror and pain, part of me wanting to vomit. But I just lay there, even when, not long afterward, he came at me again. He had been long without a wife, I now understand. Eventually he did it again—we had not exchanged a word in the meanwhile—and soon he lay over on his back and went into a sound, noisy sleep.

I lay there, crying a little, but totally passive. But the part of my mind that had screamed with nausea knew that something had to be done. Something had to be done so that this would never happen to me again. I lay there thinking, wondering. Then I got up very quietly and somehow found my way to the door. Once outside I closed it, and fumbled round the wall until I found the landing light. Then I went down to the kitchen. In the drawer where the cutlery was I looked at and felt two or three long knives. They were old but kept sharp. I remember feeling a terrible calm. I took one of them, switched off the kitchen light, and then slowly made my way upstairs. I could hear the snores of satisfied sleep, louder and louder. I opened the bedroom door and left it open, so that the dim light from the landing would assist my aim. I gently pulled back the blanket and sheet that he had over him, surveyed the plump body, then raised the knife and plunged it into his stomach, into his Cupid's dart, one, twice, again and again, pushing him back when he tried to raise himself, screaming with agony (screaming as I had wanted to scream) until finally I plunged it into his heart.

I did not look at him again. When he was quite still I took the little suitcase that he had brought up, and the clothes I had taken off before the terrible experience. I went down to the kitchen, took off my nightdress, which was hideous and sticky with our bloods, and bundled it under the sink. Then in the dim light from the landing (I wanted no light now) I found my toilet bag, took out a flannel, and washed myself in the sink. Then I put on my clothes again. I was quite calm still, but I knew I had done something unusual and I knew I could not go back to my parents' home again. I remember wondering where poor mad Lucia had stabbed her husband.

I repacked my suitcase. The handle was sticky, so I washed it clean. In the hall it was lighter. On an impulse I went into the dining room and pressed the button on the television. The picture was of naked bodies, writhing together, so I switched it off. I found my coat in the little cupboard and put it on. The jacket of Mr. Hatfield's suit was in there too, and I felt inside it and found a wallet. There was fifty pounds in it, so I took that. I knew I would need money, though I knew what nothing cost. Then I took up my little suitcase, opened the front door, and went out into the street.

It was more than three weeks before they found me. The first Sunday when we were not at church my parents wondered a little but did nothing. The second Sunday they went round to the house, but found it dark and locked. On the Monday my father walked to the paint firm for which Mr. Hatfield worked. He found that Mr. Hatfield had intended to take ten days off after the wedding, but that he had been expected back that day. The people there found my father very odd. They knew Mr. Hatfield had been about to marry a young lady he hardly knew. He had always been a meticulous man where work was concerned. By the end of the day they had called the police.

The police were hampered by the fact that my parents had no photograph of me. No visual record of my existence. They talked to them, talked to neighbors who had seen me in the garden, talked to members of the Congregation. I think they quite soon understood the situation. They realized I had nobody to go to, no place I knew where I could find refuge. They were used to the problem of homelessness. They knew I would be sleeping rough.

I greatly enjoyed those weeks, most of the time. When I left the house in Mafeking Terrace I walked through the night, following signs toward the center. I had read *Oliver Twist* and

I knew that London, real London not suburbia, was the place to lose yourself in. As light came up I often stopped to look in shopwindows, noticing prices. Later I would linger by shops with televisions on in the window, seeing the shadows of the world on the dancing screens. But now I too was in the world. Sometimes, where there were seats, I rested, watching the world go by.

How I gravitated to a place where there were others like me, people with no homes and no futures, I don't remember. But I recall a man sitting with me on a bench somewhere, very shabby and kind, and telling me that under the bridges near the Festival Hall there was "good sleeping" to be found. I had heard concerts from the Festival Hall and I suppose the name lingered in my mind. Somehow, days later, I found my way there. I had already learnt more than I had in a lifetime before. I knew about drugs. I knew about people who had in earlier years been in mental hospitals, but were now on the streets. I understood what prostitution was. I had never realized before that there were child beggars today—I had thought that was Dickens's London, long past. Now I met them, talked to them.

Around Waterloo Bridge people were very kind to me. "You're the sort of kid who doesn't know she's been born," one of them said to me. He lent me two cardboard boxes, for the nights. He taught me to take good care of my money. I met people, talked to people. Many of them came from homes much worse than mine. Many of them drank, and fought. Once I met an Asian girl who had been forced into an arranged marriage, and had run away from it. I did not exchange stories with her, though. She was very disturbed. She frightened me. Soon I was known: people called me "Jess" and smiled at me. I was with them and of them, and even ate like them—delicious slices of pizza, things called kebabs, curries from cardboard boxes, anything we could retrieve from the rubbish.

I think it was my little suitcase that marked me out for the police. Most of them had plastic carrier bags. I still had five pounds left of the fifty when a policeman came up to me in one of the windy walkways around the National Theatre and said:

"What's your name?"

"Jessica Derbyshire," I said without thinking. But I believe that even if I had thought I would have said the same. I knew a life as good as that could not last.

He was very kind—all of them were. I think enough was known about me for them to understand how it had happened. He did not summon help, or handcuff me, but walked with me to the nearest police station, talking and asking me questions. Then it all began—interviews, medical examinations, psychiatric examinations. I was in jail on remand for a while, but it wasn't really unpleasant. I learnt a lot there.

My father came to visit me. He said: "It was difficult to know what to do for the best," and "This is killing your mother." It looked as if it was killing him too, so the next day I wrote him a note saying I would understand if he did not come again, and he did not. It was odd how easily I could do without the only people I had ever really known.

The trial was funny. It was very short because, as people kept saying, "the facts were not in dispute." Everyone seemed to go out of their way to say nice things, or pitying things, about me. One of the policemen described me as "very gentle." At the end of it I was sent here.

I like it here. I've learnt a lot, as I did in prison. I don't mean school things, though I do have a teacher who comes in to teach me the usual things that most children learn in schools. She is alternately surprised at the things I don't know, and the things I do. No, I meant I'd learnt a lot from the people, the inmates and the staff. I count almost all of them as my friends, so the words "criminally insane" can't in fact be as nasty in meaning as they sound. Some of them are so disturbed that communication with them is difficult. Most of us, though, can talk about ourselves and what we have done, and help each other.

My teacher has tried to tell me about "the facts of life," but I always stop her. Those things are going to have no place in my life. I have a special friend here, a young schizophrenic, and in his good times we talk a lot, and we sit and hold hands. Nothing more, of course. The facts of life that I am interested in I started to learn when I shut the front door of the house in Mafeking Terrace, and I've gone on learning under Waterloo Bridge, in prison, and here. I know whatever happens I will never stop learning.

My psychiatrist says I may soon be ready to go out into the community again. He says it was not the intention of the court to shut me away for the rest of my life. He says it would be unwise for me to return to live at home, and I agree with him. He thinks I may be able to qualify for university, or for special training of some kind. We talk a lot about this, and I can see lots of possibilities—in fact, one delightful possibility after another: it is very difficult to make choices, with the little knowledge of the world that I have. But it's good to have someone who has confidence in me. He says things like: "You've got a real talent" and "Anyone can see that you're not a threat to the community."

I hope and pray he's right. God grant he's right.

THE HABIT OF WIDOWHOOD

*W*hen my great-great-grandmother married her first husband in 1867 the felicitations on the event from the burghers of Eastbourne were unfeigned. People were used at that time to unions between elderly men and young women, and viewed them in a light rather different from that in which they would be seen today. "Everyone v. kind," she noted in her diary. This diary was entrusted to me by my grandmother (who was "Australian respectability" personified) with a meaningful glance and instructions that it was For My Eyes Only. I am a crime writer, one of Australia's surprisingly few, and she knew it would interest me. When my great-great-grandmother's first husband died, six weeks after the marriage, people were also kind: the Victorians had a great range of euphemisms to cover procreation, childbirth, and dying, and the most common one used about his death, and that in lowered tones, was that it was difficult at his age to keep up with a young wife. My great-great-grandmother noted this down in her diary, and rather gave the game away by adding an exclamation mark.

For the diary, though usually brief, is unusually honest. Ten days before his death she had noted in that diary: "Talked to Ernest of s. bliss. V. interested." A week before his death we read: "S. bliss. Ernest *v.* excited." And on the day of his death: "E. died after s.b." Modesty forbids that I speculate on the precise nature of "s. bliss." I take it to be either secret or supreme bliss. Anyway, whatever it was, it did for poor old Ernest.

So there was Maria Halliwell, née Chalmers, a widow and

comfortably off. People said (she noted in her diary) that if she should be in an interesting condition, it was a comfort that she would be well provided for. Others said that no doubt after a suitable interval she would find a husband more her own age. But Maria was not pregnant, and after ten months of widowhood she married Charlie Ferneyhough, a respectable haberdasher, who at sixty-eight was no nearer her own age than her first.

This time I get hints from the diary that comment was less kind. What seemed prudent when done once began to seem mercenary when done a second time. She records (again with that exclamation mark!) that he was advised by his friends not to overdo things, to go steady, and so on. Such well-meaning advice met with its usual response. Three months after leading Maria down the isle of All Saints' Church, Charlie Ferneyhough was a dead man.

This time comment was far from kind. I do not know which well-meaning friend retailed it to her, but it is all there in the diary. Some ladies said there should be an autopsy, others said darkly that *that* wouldn't reveal anything. Both sexes pointed out that in the case of her first and her second husband the doctor had been summoned around eleven o'clock at night. They also pointed out that both husbands had a history of heart trouble. Oh no, they said, an autopsy wouldn't reveal anything criminal.

Maria Ferneyhough decided to move. What chance was there of a successful (in her terms) third marriage with whispers like this going around respectable Eastbourne society? She fixed on Scarborough, which had many features in common with Eastbourne—notably an aging, mainly retired population—but drew its residents from an entirely different part of the country.

Maria's third marriage, to Stanley Stalleybrass, was her longest before she finally settled—it lasted all of fifteen months. Clearly a diet of meat puddings and plum duffs and beer had not destroyed the man's hardy Yorkshire constitution. He had owned a smelting works near Barnsley, had sold up after his wife had died and moved to the coast. Maria recorded that he was "v. bored." Not for long. It would be prurient to count the number of "s. blisses" recorded in the diary after their marriage, but they certainly are frequent. It was, one feels, with a certain relief that Maria records in May 1872: "Stanley expired (after s.b.!). V. happy." I am not entirely clear whether this last comment refers to herself or to Stanley.

It would be tedious to follow Maria round for the next years of her life, for the details of her marriages as recorded in the diary are essentially similar to those which (against all the wishes of my dear grandmother) I have just recounted. She never again married two husbands in the same town, and this, I think, was prudent: though (to my knowledge) nothing criminal was ever involved, still, there was a danger of her reputation preceding her on her travels, which in fact it never did. Also it meant she could remarry quicker. So the decade saw her moving herself and her (more and more extensive) belongings to Aberdeen, St. Anne's, Leamington Spa, Edinburgh, Torquay and St. Davids, becoming successively (and after elaborate legal settlements enabling her to keep control of her fortune) Mrs. Hamish McGregor, Mrs. Alfred Dunn, Mrs. James Cadogan, Mrs. Iain MacPherson, Mrs. Lionel Blount, and Mrs. Owen Thomas. The marriages lasted various lengths of time: that to James Cadogan, for example, was over by the first night, and the diary does not record that "s.b." was involved. All the other husbands were initiated into that terrible delight, and all paid the price for it.

It was in St. Davids, that sleepy Welsh cathedral village, that Maria Thomas, as she then was, met Mr. Julius Kirkpatrick. She was very recently widowed—a condition as regular with her as a summer cold—and preparing to up sticks and find fresh woods and pastures new. Not to mention, of course, elderly lambs to be led to the slaughter. She met Mr. Kirkpatrick, she records, in the chilly, underpopulated cathedral, after Sunday service. He was, he told her, still mourning the death of his wife the previous year, and he had come to St. Davids for the loneliness of its situation, and the healthy beauty of its walks, which he hoped would add tone to his system, which had been sadly weakened by grief and a series of minor heart attacks.

He was there and then invited back to Maria's substantial house (inherited, of course) on the Square. The entries at this point in her diary were becoming longer and more revealing (she later wrote several stories of a sentimental nature for women's magazines, so perhaps it is from her that I get my bent for fiction). She records that he was "v. agreeable and well informed. Knows Edinburgh well, and Leamington Spa. Says he is sixty-one but looks yngr. Shall pursue the matter no further *here*."

The fact was that the advent in her life of Mr. Julius Kirkpatrick was an inconvenience to my great-great-grandmother's plans. She had already decided to take a cruise to Italy. One week before meeting him she had booked her passage to Naples on an India-bound steamship, which was to depart from Southampton at the beginning of March, and which would call at Le Havre, Lisbon, Marseilles, and Genoa before arriving in Naples. Maria's plans were for one month in the Italian South: she had booked a hotel for part of that time in Amalfi, and had reserved her return passage on another boat that did the India run for late April 1882. Clearly Mr. Kirkpatrick was a prospect, but no more than that. He was not to be allowed to come in the way of present happiness.

She had reckoned without the man himself. After two days at the Great Western Hotel in London ("Clothes" underlined several times in the diary) she proceeded to Southampton and went on board the *Duke of Albany,* where she found Mr. Kirkpatrick (underlined, with several exclamation marks after it, in the diary) already ensconced. They had met perhaps four or five times in her last days in St. Davids, but apparently she had him interested—so enthralled, in fact, that he had decided to pursue her. At the various stops we have "Le Havre with Mrs. Wilson, Mrs. Conway and Mr. Kirkpatrick." At Lisbon she went ashore with only Mrs. Conway and Mr. Kirkpatrick. By Marseilles she and he were alone. By Naples their friendship was a well-established thing. He went with her to Pompeii, and bought her several of the classical-headed trinkets that were the tourist fodder of the time (I have inherited a bracelet that I think must be one of these very trinkets). He escorted her up Vesuvius ("Mr. Kirkpatrick's strong arm to assist me") and even helped her choose hats and shoes. He stayed in another hotel in Amalfi while she was there, escorted her on a brief trip to Rome, and again on a weekend visit to Sicily. Clearly the friendship was more than firm, though it seems nothing was said about marriage until they were on the boat home.

There were elements in Maria's diary account of her Italian trip that I confess would have made me suspicious (but then I am a crime writer, and congenitally suspicious). The fact that Maria herself was not may be due to the fact that she was genuinely attracted to Julius Kirkpatrick. Maybe her adventurous spirit recognized its fellow. At any rate, when he proposed, the second night out of Naples, she accepted immediately—"v. happy"—and they were married four nights later in Spanish waters by the captain of the *Lahore*, the boat which they had taken, in accordance with Maria's original plans. Several times in the days that follow she records that she is "v. happy," and she describes as "enchanting" the days they spent in Lisbon and the French ports. One might almost think that her rocky marital career was over and she was finally happy, were it not that, in French waters, she recorded: "Talked to J. of s. bliss. Not v. interested."

The diary records many sayings of Julius, lists things bought, notes dinings at the captain's table and suchlike commonplaces of shipboard life until at last they docked, traveled by train to London, and settled themselves into a suite at the Great Western, intending, according to the diary, to enjoy a week in London before traveling to settle up their affairs in Pembrokeshire, though she also records that Julius was "much plagued by business matters that he is forced to attend to."

The end came three days after their return to those shores, and thanks to the fullness of the account in the diary I can perhaps exercise such fictional powers as I possess and describe the scene more fully than hitherto. It began soon after breakfast, and it was sparked off, appropriately enough, by a further reference to "s. bliss." I imagine Maria coming up behind Julius as he sat at table in their suite reading the *Daily Telegraph* (he was not a man of much education) and putting her arms around him and kissing him on the cheek.

"Is my Julius happy?"

"Deliriously happy, my dear."

"Has he everything he could wish for?"

"Very nearly everything, my dear."

"What more could he possibly want? Was he thinking of that supreme bliss that I promised to reveal to him one day?"

Mr. Kirkpatrick smiled secretively.

"No, my dear," he said, folding his paper and setting it beside his plate. "It was not that supreme bliss that you spoke to me of. In fact, I'm afraid that the rapture Mr. Thomas and Mr. MacPherson enjoyed is not destined to fall to my lot."

Maria should have known then that the game was up. She had admitted to being twice widowed, but Mr. MacPherson's was not one of the names she had mentioned.

"Perhaps you are wise, my dear . . . with your heart . . ."

"It should really have occurred to you, Maria, that a man with a weak heart does not climb Vesuvius. A weak heart would have been a severe handicap to me in my work as a private inquiry agent."

"Inquiry agent?" Maria's voice faltered.

"In vulgar parlance, a detective. One of my most interesting assignments over the past two years has been to follow you in your enterprising marital career."

"Why should you?"

"The family of the late Iain MacPherson, of Edinburgh, engaged me. The Scots, to their credit, are a suspicious race of people, and they don't take lightly to being disinherited in favor of a young wife, come from nowhere, disappearing to nowhere."

Maria's jaw set obstinately.

"I've done nothing criminal."

"Quite right, my dear. And after lengthy—and somewhat costly—investigations, that was the conclusion I was forced to report back to them. I trust they felt in some small way compensated for their expenses by the fact that the report made most interesting reading. Sad—or perhaps in one way most fortunate—that it would not be considered suitable reading for the ladies."

"When . . . did you make this report?"

"Shortly before coming to make your acquaintance in St. Davids."

Maria was reduced to silence for a moment.

"What are you going to do?"

"Well, I'm not going to indulge in any sessions designed to produce supreme bliss, that's a certainty. But you ask the wrong question, my dear. I am going to do nothing. The question is, what are you going to do?"

She drew herself up and looked him straight in the eye, as if declaring battle.

"*I?*"

"You can hardly imagine that I would sleep easy, living with a woman with such a marital history? If you have done nothing criminal as yet, still your career has strayed so breath-takingly close to the borderline that clearly you would cross it the moment you thought it would suit your purposes to do so. The question is, then, where are you to go?"

"*I* to go? I should have thought—"

"I fear that in this case you have not thought nearly enough, my dear. I have already wired Davies, the lawyer in St. Davids, that the house there is to be sealed. I know you have bank accounts both in London and in St. Davids, and I have set my lawyers on to make sure you are refused access to these. There you may see the beauty of our romantic ship-board marriage, my dear. You were unable to consult with lawyers and to arrange the usual settlements and jointures."

"But . . . there's protection now for married women! Protection against men like you!"

"Ah—you refer to the Married Women's Property Act—if I may say so, a wise and long-overdue measure. This is a milestone year for the female sex. No doubt you followed the debates and the newspaper discussions with interest. Alas, those were but debates, were but discussions. Unfortunately—and this really *is* unfortunate for you—the bill has not yet become law, is not expected to receive royal assent until the summer. Your property, my dear, is mine and mine alone."

"This is monstrous!"

"You see now the urgency as well as the cunning of my plan. But I am not an unreasonable person. Legally you may have claim to little more than the clothes you stand up in. Upon compassionate grounds I will certainly allow you to take all your clothes and personal effects—jewelry and suchlike things. Pity you always went for money in the bank rather than portable property, don't you think? But I'll be generous: I'll add a sum of ready money. Shall we say five hundred pounds? Yes, I think that would do nicely. Five hundred pounds—on condition that you do the one thing that will make my present happiness complete: remove yourself and all trace of you from this hotel by nightfall."

I do not know how long my great-great-grandmother stormed, fumed, counterattacked, protested, pleaded, but I do know she was out of that hotel by nightfall. And I do know that before many weeks had passed she was on the boat to Australia—no doubt feeling that only such a place was sufficiently remote for her to resume her career without the attentions of Mr. Kirkpatrick spoiling her schemes.

It was a mistaken choice. Australia was then still a young country, a country of young men making their fortunes. Old men who had made theirs were not thick on the ground, as they were in the seaside and spa towns of Great Britain. But my great-great-grandmother was a great believer in the institution of marriage, and had never found it wanting. Within a year of landing she had married (with what legality it is perhaps best not to inquire) George Atherton, an ironmonger of Sydney two years younger than herself, a vigorous man, by all accounts, and one who could stand any amount of supreme bliss. Though by then she was in her later thirties, she soon produced two sons, and thus established the line of Athertons who have figured prominently in the history of New South Wales and Australia. It was a transformation into respectability, into social prominence, that was remarkable even by Australian standards.

But there is one more fact about my great-great-grandmother Maria Atherton, and I record it without comment. Though the Athertons were moderately prosperous, their place in the Sydneyocracy was gained after she received a legacy of seventy thousand pounds, a great sum in those days, from a retired New England grazier. The will paid tribute to her as one of the most remarkable women in Sydney, and added that she had made an old man very happy.

POST MORTEM

*T*hroughout my father's funeral my mother sternly kept back her emotion. At home afterwards, with the relatives and the top people from the factory, she was controlled, almost gracious, though often I noticed her eyes downturned, her mouth working. Only when the stragglers had been seen from the door and the last car had driven away did she come back into the lounge, let out a great whoop of triumph, and throw her black hat in the air.

"Hooray! Shot of him at last!"

I looked at her disapprovingly. There were no neighbors to hear, for The Maples is set in extensive grounds, but in the kitchen was Mrs. Mottram, who had prepared and served the funeral bakemeats. I pointed meaningfully in that direction.

My mother leaned forward in her chair.

"I don't give a monkey's fart for Mrs. Mottram."

But she said it in a low hiss, which showed that she had taken my point.

Now she started moving restlessly around the room. When our fellow mourners were here she had pressed food on them but had eaten nothing herself. Now she greedily sampled everything, eating voraciously as if she had ordered the lavish spread precisely with this moment in mind.

"These vol-au-vents are delicious. No one can say we didn't give him a good send-off. . . . I wonder if I should phone the solicitor."

"Of *course* you shouldn't. How would it look?" Seeing this

argument carried no weight with her, I added: "Anyway, you know Mr. Blore is away. Otherwise he would have been here at the funeral. He wouldn't want any underling to deal with it. He said he'd be back tomorrow."

My mother's mouth grimaced into a little moue.

"But how on earth are we going to get through the rest of the day?"

In the end I took her for a long drive, well away from Rotherham, where the McAtee works and the family home are situated. In a small Derbyshire pub she got thoroughly sloshed on her favorite gin slings, and that kept her happy till morning.

It was as much as I could do to stop her ringing Mr. Blore immediately after breakfast. "Solicitors don't get to work at nine o'clock," I said. As it was, she made an awful impression by ringing at twenty past, and finding he was not due in till ten-fifteen. She finally spoke to him at twenty past ten, and though she conducted her end of the conversation with the sort of decorum she had shown at the funeral, when she put down the phone she seemed oddly dissatisfied.

"When I said we had a copy of the will here, he said: 'Well, we'll discuss all that tomorrow.'"

That should have told me.

My mother dressed the part next day, which was a relief. She is inclined to use a too bright lipstick for a woman of her age, and an inappropriate nail varnish. People say she is vulgar and grasping, but we get on all right. Not because I am vulgar and grasping, but because I like a quiet life. Anyway, her black was irreproachable.

Mr. Blore treated us with the utmost respect, as no doubt he always did treat grieving relatives, whether he liked them or not (and in the case of my mother he certainly didn't). He ushered us to seats, offered dry, solicitorial condolences to my mother, inquired of me if the funeral arrangements had been satisfactory. We fed him back with muted platitudes. Then he sat back in his chair and let us have it.

"But that's bloody impossible!" screamed my mother, her mask slipping badly. "How could there be a later will? He made this one just before he became ill. He had no chance—"

"Nevertheless he made one."

My mother thought.

"Mrs. Mottram. I'd bet my bottom dollar—"

Mr. Blore inclined his head noncommittally.

"And I believe there were days when you had other cleaning staff in . . ."

"Spick and Span. They gave the house a thorough clean every fortnight. I always went out when they came. . . . Witnesses. . . . I must have been mad."

"And your husband had access to a typewriter."

For those little notices to the workforce—exhortations, pep talks, ironic little comments on slackness—which I had dutifully pinned up on the notice board, and which had aroused more derision than respect since he was no longer on the shop floor to enforce his will.

"Oh God, yes, he had a typewriter," said my mother impatiently, the social veneer having been cast off long since. "But this new will—"

"Is by and large the same as the old one. I need not go over the provisions of that. Unfortunately the most substantial clause, the one leaving the works and the bulk of the fortune to you, with reversion to Mr. Maurice McAtee"—he nodded in my general direction, and I got the strongest possible sense that he was enjoying himself—"is changed."

"Yes. Hurry *up*, man."

"He expresses the hope that Mr. Maurice will be allowed to remain in his present job, as he has been a conscientious works manager, but he doubts he has the drive or flair to head the enterprise. He therefore names Mr. Henry McAtee—"

"Harry! But he hated Harry! He cast him off!"

"A change of mind, I fear. Mr. Henry is to inherit both the factory and the residual fortune."

"You're joking! What about me?"

"You, madam, are not named in the will."

"But that's impossible! That's not legal!"

"It is perfectly legal, madam. A man or woman may leave his possessions to whomsoever he pleases. It *is* possible for you, Mrs. McAtee, to sue in the High Court for a more adequate provision. Normally they would award you the sort of settlement you might have expected had you and your husband divorced. Doubtless you will consider this course. Nevertheless, I have to warn you that there are certain—er—allegations in your husband's covering letter to me that would have to come out in court, and which might well—er—lead the court to take a very different view of the matter."

It really broke my mother up. In the car going home she kept sobbing and wailing: "After all I'd done." It was notable that she did not add "for him." That wasn't what she meant at all. As we neared The Maples she muttered in a vitriolic whisper: "I'll strangle his bloody pigeons."

For my father had had a love of racing pigeons, which my mother said was a sentimental relic of his working-class origins. Me, I think he genuinely loved the things. More than he did us. As soon as we got home my mother went out through the kitchen to execute her threat, but she found it a good deal more difficult than she expected. She ended up with her frustration still boiling over, and nothing more to show for her efforts than a few pigeon feathers scattered around the kitchen garden.

My brother Harry arrived home the next day. That in itself showed that he had been forewarned, or rather forepromised. The solicitor had said he would write on the day he spoke to us. Harry was wearing a sober suit. His usual sort of dress was casual-sexy, in keeping with his image of himself as a trendy pop-star type. He had no doubt bought the suit in preparation for his good fortune. Typical of Harry that he should have spared himself the bother of the funeral.

He was met at the door by Mrs. Mottram, who showed him into the lounge. "Awfully sad occasion," he kept muttering, as he kissed my mother and shook my hand, his eyes sparkling with pleasure the while. When Mrs. Mottram had retired to the kitchen he threw himself into an armchair and let out a great bellow of laughter.

"Oh, what a turn-up for the book. If you two could only see yourselves! You look like dogs who've just had a particularly juicy bone pinched from under their noses."

My mother could barely refrain from buffeting him around the head, as she so often had done in his delinquent childhood. But that day we observed the decencies, she and I. Mrs. Mottram was around all day, with a fair idea of what was going on but an incomplete one. We had no desire—my mother and I had no desire—to feed her raging hunger for gossip material. We ate the meal she cooked us decorously, while Harry fed us a (doubtless censored) version of what he had been doing in the seven years since Father had shown him the door of The Maples and told him (erroneously) that that was the last time he would see the inside of it.

The next day Harry once again donned his sober suit and once again assumed his sober manner, and he and I went down to the factory. Changes made in the last few years made it necessary for him to be shown around it, but I had no intention of doing that myself and watching him gloat. I handed him over to the foreman and went on with my own work. Harry was remembered from the old days and thoroughly disliked (he had done the "boss's son" act to an outrageous degree, and treated everyone from floor cleaner to foreman with contempt). Now he listened with a display of humility, but as the day wore on I heard him say things like "That will have to be changed," or "I'm sure we can devise a better system than that," or—most ominously—"What seems to be needed is a daring policy of expansion to pull us out of the doldrums." This last brought visions to my mind of lunatic schemes followed by a spectacular bankruptcy. I had told no one at the factory of Harry's good fortune, but by the end of the day the whole workforce must have guessed.

As he left, my brother said to the foreman: "I'll be in at nine and doing a full day's work tomorrow. Start as you mean to go on—eh?"

Mrs. Mottram was off that day. My mother cooked a dinner of all the things my brother particularly disliked. He maintained a flow of unabating geniality through it all, and treated me to a long account of all the changes that he intended to initiate at the McAtee works.

"Father himself saw the need for change," he concluded, over the spotted dick, which he merely picked at. "That's why he put me in charge."

"Then it's odd he never broached the subject to me," I said sourly.

"Ah, but you're not the boy for change, are you, Morrie? 'Do as we've always done,' that's your motto. Tried and tested methods. But tried and tested methods don't do in the age of the computer. Industry has to develop and expand or go to the wall. Those were Father's very words."

"I don't remember them," I said.

"Well, you wouldn't, would you?" Harry grinned, his habitual self-satisfaction oozing from every pore. "They were in a letter to me—the one in which he explained the new . . . arrangements. He was very considerate: told me to wait a day or two after the funeral before I came down, to give you two time to get used to the change in your fortunes. Otherwise, of course, my natural instinct would have been to pay my last respects to the old boy." He crumpled his napkin beside his plate and stood up. "It was an interesting letter altogether."

That silenced us. Somehow, though he said it casually, it was as if every word was italicized. The way he looked at us, first Mother and then me, added to the effect. He took a folder of facts and figures from the factory and went up to his bedroom.

My mother was devastated, as well she might be.

"He'll have to go," she said. "We'll have to get rid of him."

"Are you mad? With us the two obvious suspects? You don't even know whether he's made a will or not. He may have a wife, a live-in girlfriend, a child. Then where would we be? I suppose if you *want* to spend the rest of your life doing Open University courses with Myra Hindley . . ."

That silenced her. I think she noticed that I said "you," not "we." It was perhaps cruel of me to rub in my separateness from her by adding: "If it's not a question of that already."

The next morning Harry merely snatched a slice of toast on the wing, as it were, and gulped down a cup of tea. Mother and I ate in silence. The reason was that we had both of us heard Harry, while he was in the bathroom, going through the medicine cabinet. He could have found nothing, of course, but it made us uneasy. So did the fact that the reason for his lateness to breakfast was that he was having a long talk with Mrs. Mottram in the kitchen. He drove off in his own car to the factory, and I heard little of him during the day, though I registered the fact that he had already put the shop stewards' backs up—unions like change even less than management, and Harry's manner was not an emollient one.

His needling of us began in earnest that night. Mrs. Mottram's hours were staggered: sometimes she came in early, cooked lunch, and left around teatime; at others she came late and stayed to cook the dinner. That night she should have been off, but stayed late "to oblige Mr Harry." Harry fetched his own plate from the kitchen, tasted it, and then said:

"Marvelous. Tastes just like steak and kidney pie should."

That was all, but that was enough. The next evening, when my mother was cooking the dinner again, Harry ostentatiously phoned for a table at Rotherham's best restaurant. It was all show, of course, all a battle of nerves: he had eaten my mother's cooking on the second evening. But it was a battle that my mother and I did not feel we were winning.

He had been in the saddle at the works for several days—and faces there were getting grimmer, and I was imagining financial disaster staring us in the face—when he took the opportunity of one of Mrs. Mottram's dinners to come a little further out into the open.

"Bumped into a chap I used to know today."

"Oh?"

"Jack Lippincott. Used to be at school with him. He's a dispensing chemist with Boots these days."

"Oh?" I managed to keep the quaver out of my voice. Why, in any case, should there be one? I didn't know what Mother had got up to. Or perhaps that should read: I didn't *know* what Mother had got up to.

"Useful knowing a chemist. He's doing a little job for me."

My mother said nothing. This was her new policy: to say nothing beyond conversational banalities to Harry. I didn't see that it could get her anywhere, but then I couldn't think of any policy that would get her anywhere.

There was nothing to do but wait.

Two days later he took up the subject over sherry (actually Harry was drinking beer; he was not a beer man, but he drank cans of it, no doubt to make the point that opened bottles can be tampered with).

"I got the report on that little job I gave Jack Lippincott to do today."

This time both Mother and I kept silent.

"I took him some bottles of Father's Polifexin."

"That's nonsense. You couldn't have."

That was my mother—it was out before she could remember her policy.

"Couldn't have? Because you put them in the garbage bin? Actually Mrs. Mottram retrieved them before the dustman came."

He smiled round at us, like a little boy before he starts torturing a bird. We kept quiet. It never does the bird much good to squawk.

"And he tells me—roughly what I expected—that while two of the eight bottles do indeed contain Polifexin, the other six contain a mixture that he can only guess at: he thinks there's lemon juice, Cointreau, a patent cough linctus and maybe other things too. 'It doesn't taste the same,' my father said in his letter. You tried to make it so it did, but it didn't quite work."

"This is ridiculous," said my mother vitriolically. "If I was trying to poison your father—"

"I'm not suggesting you were doing anything of the sort. You were withholding the medicine he needed after his first stroke."

"Either way, why didn't he protest to Mrs. Mottram? Ask her to help, send for the police? Come to that, why didn't he say anything to Dr. Craigie? He came seldom enough, God knows, considering your father's standing in the community, but he did come."

"I've thought about that. Mrs. Mottram had suspicions of her own, which is why she retrieved the bottles. She tells me that there were a lot of lemons bought that she couldn't account for because no one in the house likes them, or uses them in tea or in gin and tonics. But you're right: Father could have told her of his suspicions, or the doctor. . . . I have a theory about that, anyway."

"What?" I asked.

"He wanted to die. After all, what sort of existence was it, stuck up in his bedroom there, after the active life he'd led— running the factory, playing cricket, later bowls, walking a lot, seeing to his pigeons and racing them. No, he must have known all those things were of the past. He wanted it over with."

"He had only to swallow a bottle of aspirin," said my mother, in that bitter voice she had used when speaking of my father since his death—and before it, come to think of it. "There was one by his bed. God knows I hoped often enough that he would. That would have saved us all a lot of trouble."

"I'm not sure he had any desire to save you trouble. Because he must quite soon have got a suspicion of what you were trying to do. Father—remember, Morrie?—always had a wonderful sense of humor."

That was true enough. Throughout our childhood he was full of conundrums, practical jokes, and jolly japes—until, that is, he saw that I always missed the point, Harry hated anything in which he might be made to look a fool, and my mother would remain stony-faced on principle. Being the one with the sense of humor in our family was about as rewarding as being the one with the sense of humor in Mrs. Thatcher's cabinet.

"I remember," I said.

"So he played a game with you. He decided to let Mother go ahead with her little plot, but to arrange an unexpected ending for her." Harry put down his beer mug and smiled around. "He was a joker, our dad."

The awful thing was the sense of helplessness. We were wounded birds at the mercy of Harry, the cruel cat. Or perhaps it was my father who was the cat? That thought was to my mother the bitterest thought of all. She had fought my father all her life and now to find herself, after his death, unexpectedly his powerless victim—that was hard. But what *was* there we could do against that relishing glint in Harry's eyes?

He waited. Like all cruel cats, he played it slow. He ate out a lot, thoroughly enjoyed his new position at the works, and just occasionally made remarks like "Remember, if you try anything against me, you'd have to do away with Mrs. Mottram as well. Then of course there's my friend Lippincott. Quite a little bloodbath you'd have to undertake...."

These thoughts, I'm sure, had already occurred to my mother. I tried not to discuss anything with her. I preferred not to know. It was bad enough during my father's illness, suspecting.

It was more than a week later, one Saturday at the end of breakfast, that Harry opened fire again.

"I think it's about time you told me your plans."

"Plans?"

"Yes, plans. I shall be needing this house. My girlfriend will be coming up here in a week or two's time. She'll make a wonderful hostess for the firm—better than it's ever had. She has a touch of class, has Sheila. So you two had better be thinking of moving on."

"But I've no mon—"

Harry ignored our mother and turned to me.

"You, Morrie, I've decided to keep on as works manager. That seems to be what Father intended, and he's right: it's the sort of plodding job you're just about up to. And after all, I don't think you ever *knew*, did you?" I sat there dumbly. "I don't think Mother would ever have confided in you, not explicitly. . . . You may have had your suspicions, though, eh, Morrie? A little idea that something was going on? But as long as nothing was said, nothing that made you even remotely into an accomplice, then you were in the clear. But anyway I've decided to keep you on in the job. *Provided* it's clear you serve me with the most complete, unquestioning loyalty, and carry out the new policies I'm working on to the letter. Loyalty is always important, but when it's family working together it's quite vital. I'm not going to tolerate an alternative power base in my own firm. Is that quite clear?"

I nodded miserably. He turned suavely to our mother.

"You were saying, Mother?"

"I have no money."

"I believe there is such a thing as National Assistance, or Income Support, or whatever damned name they use these days. Personally I'm against state charity, as I'm sure you are. It saps the initiative. There are plenty of jobs a woman of your age can do—jobs in the service industries, cafeteria jobs, cleaning jobs. Not well paid, of course, or pleasant, but as the saying goes: beggars can't be choosers."

"I've nowhere to live."

"Haven't you got yourself on the Council list? They probably have a nice little flat in one of the high-rises. People don't like living in them, but I'm sure you'd find it perfectly pleasant. It's only a penthouse flat under another name, isn't it? Or perhaps Morrie would let you live with him for a while. If I know Morrie he's got a bit of money saved, so he'll certainly be able to walk into a nice little house or flat. You'll have the rest of your lives to talk things over."

The post plopped through the door, and Harry went to fetch it while still talking.

"You notice, Mother, I've said nothing about going to the police. . . . Circular from the RSPB. Now *that's* a charity we can cut out. . . . I rather think I ought to go to the police. My own father cut off permanently. I'd be fully justified. But I'm a tenderhearted guy. Didn't know that, did you, Mother? Well, I am. I don't say I never *will* go to them: doubts gnawing in my mind—that's only one of the lines I could take. But for the moment, and depending on your good behavior, I won't go yet." He chuckled. "I don't think that's what Father would have wanted. I'm sure he expected me to dob you in. But what he didn't realize was, I'd have a sort of fellow feeling with you. Because if I'd still been here, I'd have done exactly the same as you. Maybe we'd have been partners, you and me, Mother. Morrie's a born sitter-out, but I'm a doer. Maybe we'd have sat here and planned it all together. So though I may be going against his wishes . . ."

He talked on, loving it. I was still sitting at the table. Suddenly my eye caught the envelope. I started to say: "But this isn't a circular," but bit it back. The letter was individually addressed, and to Henry McAtee. A sudden conviction concerning my father's sense of humor washed through me.

Feverishly I picked it up and opened it. It was on the notepaper of the Royal Society for the Protection of Birds.

"Dear Mr. McAtee," it read. "In accordance with your father's instructions in the covering letter, we have waited for a fortnight after his funeral before opening the will he sent us. As you will see from the enclosed copy . . ."

I was glad that at last I had managed to see one of my father's jokes.

SOLDIER, FROM THE
WARS RETURNING

I have a photograph of my grandfather—my real grandfather—in the uniform of the King's Own Yorkshiremen, taken on leave in 1917, when he had finished his weeks of training and was about to be sent to France. He gazes out into the camera—young, confident, even cocky. I have been told that young soldiers were encouraged to have such pictures taken, ostensibly on the grounds that they instilled smartness and pride in the regiment, in fact because their officers suspected that the photograph would soon be all that the family had to remember them by.

But this was not the case with my grandfather, Jimmy Larkins. He bucked the statistics. He served in France and Belgium for eighteen months and only sustained a minor wound in the final push of the autumn of 1918. He also survived the flu epidemic of 1919, that final dirty trick of the President of the Immortals. On his demob he got a job as a baker's roundsman in his hometown of Armley, and he put the war behind him.

On the surface, at least. I do not believe that any normally sensitive person could go through those hellish years entirely unchanged. He had not sunk, suffocating, into the mud, he had not been shot as he clambered over the ridge of his trench, but he had seen hundreds who had, had known them, perhaps loved them with the comradely love of soldiers. What Jimmy Larkins would have been like if he had grown up normally in peacetime no one can now know. As it was, he seems to have come home with an urge to make up for lost time, perhaps even to live a little for the lads who had not come home.

And there were plenty of women and girls in the Armley area who were willing to help him do it: women whose husbands had not come home, girls whose potential husbands were remembered collectively on Armistice Day, women whose husbands had come home crippled or haunted—and, indeed, women whose husbands followed the normal Northern working-class tradition that the husband's leisure time was spent boozing with his mates while his wife stayed home to cook, clean and mind the children. There were lonely, unhappy, dissatisfied women aplenty in Jimmy Larkins's Armley, and he did his best to bring a little joy into their lives. It was rumored that at moments of climax he would cry: "That's one from Archie Hoddle!" or "That's for you, Robbie Robson!"— all the names of mates of his who had never come home from France to sow their own wild oats.

This was a rumor, as I say, for this was not the sixties, when privacy and reticence were dirty words and happiness was thought to flow from endless talk about one's sexual proclivities and activities. This was the twenties, when you kept yourself to yourself, and all but the outcast families maintained a wall of respectability between themselves and the outside world.

But if the ladies did not discuss among themselves what Jimmy did or did not say when he was reaching climax with them, they did show their knowledge of his activities obliquely, in jokes. "What she needs is a visit from Jimmy Larkins," they would say of a sour spinster, or "Serve your man right if you started asking Jimmy Larkins in," they would tell a neglected wife. After a time they started hinting that they could see his features in the babies that were born. "I don't like the look of that snub nose," they would say, or "Who does that high forehead remind me of?" Thus, in ritual jokes, did the women of Armley reveal their awareness of my grandfather's doings in the neighborhood without their ever acknowledging that he had brought to them personally, along with the bread, that other staff of life.

The women, as I say, could joke about it. Some, no doubt, wanted more from the relationship and became emotional and demanding, but Jimmy had his ways of avoiding commitment. When asked why he had never married he always said briefly: "It wouldn't be fair." I take him to have been good-hearted and promiscuous, fleeing mentally from the blackness of those months in France. For a time, perhaps, even the men of Armley understood.

But the men never treated it as a joke, and as the twenties turned into the thirties they found that the whole business was becoming very sour indeed. These men had a pride of paternity as fierce as that of any aristocrat, and they added a sense of *possession*—exclusive possession—of a wife that boded ill both for the wives themselves and for Jimmy. The fact that they spent their evenings and weekends in pubs gave no sort of leeway to the wives they left cooped up with a brood within four walls. Their suspicion and anger found their own form, and it was not jocular. "Someone should take a knife to that randy bastard," they would mutter into their pint mugs, or "I'd like to get that bugger up a back alley some dark night—I'd know what to do to him."

Their rage and frustration were dynastic too: they looked at their children, and particularly their sons, and they wondered if they were the fathers. They studied features, even pondered their characters and tastes, and wondered "where they got that from," as if that were a scientific study and could give them certainty one way or the other. In the end they usually subsided into a boiling uncertainty which found occasional outlets in violence to their wives or their offspring.

Usually but not always. They were simple men with strong, not always rational, feelings and a fierce pride. Their manhood was their most precious possession, and if they felt it impugned they became enraged. They loved certainties and feared doubt. To live in uncertainty, permanently, was to them a condition barely tolerable. Some of them, discussing the matter over the years, first in hints and ambiguities, later with angry directness, determined to do something about it. There were six of them: Walter Abbot, Fred Walmsley, Bill Hoggett, Mickey Turner, Harry Colton and Peter Huggins. They are names that still crop up in Armley pubs and clubs, because the crime was a local sensation, something much more than a nine-day wonder, and the men—and, inevitably, their wives— became the objects of finger-pointing hushed discussion that lasted the rest of their lives.

In spite of the violent prognostications of the Armley men they did not decide to castrate Jimmy. Something in them shrank from that, as it did not shrink from murder. They decided to kill him in such a way that all of them must be under suspicion but no one would be able to decide which had done it.

What may seem odd, even ironic, today is the game they chose as a cover for the murder. Bowls has nowadays a gentle, middle-class, elderly image: it is a game that is played when physical powers have declined and all passions are spent. But many workingmen in the thirties played bowls: a relaxing game after a day of hard, physical work. Four of the men were good players, and the pub where Jimmy Larkins had his pint or two after work was only a hundred yards or so from the Armley Bowling Club. So one autumn evening the six of them turned up, casually and separately, in the Wagon of Hay, bought Jimmy an extra pint, and finally set out for a game of bowls with Jimmy as umpire. Whether Jimmy, as he rolled off with them, was secretly cock-a-hoop that he had cuckolded every one of them, I do not know. I hope not—hope he regarded his relations with their womenfolk in a different light from that. But we shouldn't try to endow the people of a past age with our own ideological baggage.

The facts of the case were always simple. They played, in the failing light, a game of bowls. At some point in the game Jimmy went off, as he was bound to do, to go to the small public lavatory by the green. The other men claimed they had not noticed when he left, nor who had gone to the lavatory immediately afterwards. They had all relieved themselves at some stage of the game, but they had not gone into the cubicle. They had finished playing without Jimmy—it was a friendly game, and an umpire was not necessary—and had then gone home. Jimmy's body was found next morning in the cubicle. He had been stabbed, and the old raincoat which had been used to protect his murderer from blood had then been thrown over him.

Those were the facts, and no one ever got very far behind or beyond them. The next day the police began a series of interrogations of the men—and, to a buzz of local gossip, their wives. The men stuck doggedly to their story: they didn't remember when Jimmy had left the green, and they didn't remember who had gone to the lavatory after him. They had assumed he had gone home, and had gone on with the game without thinking any more about him. They never pretended to have seen other men or women on or around the green, for, though they were hard men, even brutal, they were fair. At one point, three weeks after the murder, the police charged them all with conspiracy to murder, but they could find no evidence that the men had conspired, so, fearing a fiasco in court, they soon dropped the charge. And so there it was: six men, all with the opportunity and the identical motive for murder. The police, and everyone in Armley, knew that one of the men had done the deed, but no one knew which.

I must be one of the few people alive who do know. I was told by my grandmother, Florrie Abbot, sitting in her little kitchen in Armley, while upstairs in the bedroom they had shared the man I called my grandfather was dying painfully of cancer. She told me the story in low, angry tones, interrupted by tears, none of them for the dying man upstairs.

My Son, My Son

*L*eonard Parkin planned the birth of his son for the seventeenth of October. He was going down to London for a management conference on the sixteenth, and there was a social event of the usual dreary kind in the evening, which he decided to leave early so as to enjoy all the exciting terror of the beginning of labor. The main conference was in the morning, but the afternoon was free and he was not planning to take the train home to Peterborough until after the evening rush hour. John Julian would be born in the afternoon.

At the evening reception, held in an anonymous hotel on the fringes of Bloomsbury, Len was rather abstracted, but in the general atmosphere of wine fumes and grabs for canapés nobody noticed. They didn't notice either when he first slipped away to the gentlemen's, then left the hotel altogether. Len was liked, but he wasn't much noticed.

Back in the Great Northern, his usual hotel, Len put the chain on his door and lay happily on his bed. He wondered whether to crack the little bottle of champagne in the room fridge, but he decided that champagne wasn't right, not for the labor. He would have a bottle of wine later on. What he wanted now was just to lie back on his bed and imagine it.

Marian, after all these months, feeling the first pains. The look she gave him, the certainty in her eyes and in his. "I think it's starting"—those time-honored words which would grant Marian kinship with the millions of other women who had used them. What would he do? He would go over and kiss her tenderly on the forehead, then he would run to the telephone and ring the well-rehearsed number. The waiting, the waiting! Another terrible pain, just as he saw the flashing light of the ambulance drawing up outside.

He went with her, of course, the two of them silent in the back, he letting her grip his hand tighter and tighter as the agony came, receded, then came again. Then the arrival at the hospital, the stretchered rush to the maternity ward, he always by her side.

He lay there for two hours, picturing the scene, filling in small details, living through Marian's pain and her thrilled anticipation, being there with him beside her. Then he got up and poured himself some wine. It was good, but somehow as he drank, the scene became less vivid. Natural, of course, but disappointing. He wouldn't have a drink tomorrow. He needed to be at his most alert tomorrow.

After the morning's business, all the representatives at the conference for the people in the confectionery business were free to do what they pleased, and they all dispersed to boozy gatherings in pubs, on shopping sprees to Harrods and Oxford Street, or on unspecified business in Soho. Leonard went to Hyde Park and lay under a tree in the sun. There his mind winged him back effortlessly to the maternity ward, and to himself sitting there by Marian, helping her through her labor. In real life, he suspected, he would have refused to be there with his wife, or been there only reluctantly, being faint-hearted about that sort of thing. But in his imagination he could make the labor terrible but short, and he could cut to the magical moment when the baby was born, to his touching it, blotchy and screaming, to his seeing it for the first time in Marian's arms—no, not it, but *him*, John Julian Parkin, his son and heir.

The day was sunny and he lay there, rapturous, ecstatic, more intensely alive then he had ever been. For hours he lay savoring the sensations: the sound, the smell, the touch of his newborn son. Then he walked all the way to the station, got his case out of Left Luggage, and caught the train home. On the hour's journey he invented little embellishments, made more vivid the picture of his son's face. It had been a perfect day.

It was late when he finally got home, and Marian was preparing the supper.

"Have a good conference?" she asked.

"Very good indeed," he said, kissing her, feeling a sudden spurt of love for his practical, commonsensical, infertile wife. The strongest feeling in her down-to-earth heart was her passionate love for him, made poignant by her inability to have children. He could never share the birth of their son with her. Her incomprehension would have killed him stone dead. Probably she would even have felt hurt, rebuked, and any blaming was far from his thoughts.

John Julian grew apace in the months that followed, but no quicker than a natural child would have. Leonard was strict about that. As he grew, his picture became sharper in his father's mind: how much hair he had at birth, and what color it was; how quickly he acquired more; the precise shape of his snub nose; how he looked when he smiled. Naturally there were setbacks and worries: Len would sometimes enliven a long car journey on business by imagining bouts of colic or the worries of teething. The great landmark joys he usually kept for some business trip which would involve a night away from home. Then, as on the first occasion, he would slip away as early as he decently could from whatever function or meeting he was obliged to attend, shut himself in his hotel room, and re-create his mental world around the son that had been born to him. The pictures were so vivid—of Marian breast-feeding their boy, of his first words, the first tentative steps—that they became part of his existence, the most cherished part.

Sometimes it became quite difficult to make the transition from the imaginary to the real world. He would come through his front door with memories still crowding around him and expect to see Marian cradling John Julian in her arms, or playing with him on the floor by the fire. Then he would have to drag himself down to earth and inquire about her day rather than John Julian's, tell her what he'd been doing, not what he'd been imagining. For Marian remained the commonsense, slightly drab woman who reserved her greatest intensity for their lovemaking, while the Marian of his imagination had blossomed with motherhood, had become altogether more sophisticated and curious about the world. She had given up her job in the chain store to be with their boy, but Len never resented sharing him with her because certain times and certain duties were by common agreement his and his alone.

He was a healthy boy, that was a blessing. He played well with the other children in the street, and on the one morning in the week when he went to play group, the leader commented on his nice disposition. Len started to imagine futures for him, though all the time with the proviso in his mind that of course John Julian would do exactly what he wanted to do when the time came for him to choose. He was an active, open-air child, but Len didn't want him to be a professional athlete. It was too short and too limiting a life. But he'd be a very good amateur. Len always said when the Olympic Games were on that it was a pity the facilities weren't used afterward for a Games for *real* amateurs. Perhaps by the time John Julian was a young man they would be, and he would compete—maybe as a middle-distance runner, or perhaps a pole-vaulter.

His real work would surely be something where he could use his brain. There was no disputing that he had one, he was so forward. Len didn't fancy his becoming a doctor, as so many parents hoped for their children, and certainly he didn't want a surgeon son. Still, he would like something that brought with it a degree of prestige. He finally settled on Oxford and a science degree, with a fellowship to follow, and a succession of brilliant research projects.

But that was what he hoped for. The boy's future was for him to decide, though he knew John Julian would want to talk it through with both his parents before he made his decision. John Julian was rather an old-fashioned sort of boy.

Meanwhile there was a real highlight in his life coming up: his first day at school. Marian had agreed—the Marian in his mind had agreed—that he should take him on his first day. She would be taking him day in, day out after that, she said: that would be her pleasure. It was only right that Len should have the joy of the first day. One of the firm's confectionery factories was near Scarborough, and Len usually visited it once a year. He arranged to go in early September—Tuesday the fourth, the day that school started for five-year-olds in his area. He booked a good hotel in the upper part of the town and he went off with a head brimming with happy anticipation.

He got through the inspection and consultations well enough. He had had to train himself over the past five years not to be abstracted, not to give only half his attention to matters of that kind: after all, it would never do for John Julian's father to be out of a job. When he was asked by one of the local managers to dinner with him and his wife that evening, Len said with every appearance of genuine regret that unfortunately he was committed to visiting "a relative of the wife's." In fact, when the day's work was done, he went back to the hotel, then took the funicular railway down to the sands. In a rapturous walk along the great stretch of beach he imagined what his day would have been.

John Julian was excited, of course. Immensely excited. He had dressed himself and was down to breakfast by half past seven, and when his father and his mother smiled at his enthusiasm he said that he had to pack his schoolbag, though in fact he had done it the night before, and packed and unpacked it for days before that. When they set out from the front door Leonard was immensely touched when John Julian reached up and took his hand, conscious that he needed guidance and protection at this great moment of his life. At the gate he turned to wave to Mummy at the door, then took Len's hand again for the ten minutes' walk to the school, sometimes shouting to friends of his own age who were also with their parents on their first day at school. At the school gate John Julian looked up at his father to say as clearly as if he had used words: "You *will* come in as you promised, won't you?" So Len went in, as most of the parents did, knowing the new children's classroom from the introductory tour the week before. Soon the children were mingling, playing, and discovering their new world, and the parents, with conspiratorial glances at each other, could slip away. The wind buffeted Len's face as he walked back to the funicular and thought what a wrench it was to leave him, and what a happiness to walk home with some of the other parents, talking parents' talk, swapping tales of achievements and setbacks, hopes and prospects.

Back in the hotel room, Len imagined his day, going over things with Marian, wondering what John Julian was doing, speculating whether he was getting on well with his teacher ("She seemed such a nice woman"). As with most parents, such speculation was endless and self-feeding, and Len decided to save the fetching of his son from school as a delicious treat for next day.

His work at the factory, his talk in the canteen, was dispatched with his usual efficiency. By late afternoon he was on the train to York, and then on the Inter-City to Peterborough, gazing sightlessly at the rolling English countryside. His son had run into his arms at the school gates, almost incoherent in his anxiety to tell his father everything about his day. Len had sat him on the wall of the playground to give him a few minutes to get his breath and tell him all the most important points. Then they had walked home hand in hand, John Julian still chattering nineteen to the dozen as he retrieved from his memory more facts and encounters of vital interest in his young life. Marian was waiting at the door and the whole thing was to do again—all the day's events recounted, all the jumble of impressions and opinions rolled out again for her.

Marian in fact was not home when he got in. She was still at her night-school class in nineteenth-century history. Len made himself a sandwich, poured a glass of milk, and sat by the kitchen table gazing out at the twilit garden, smiling to himself as he went through the excitements and joys of his day. He did not hear his wife let herself in through the front door. He did not realize she stood for some moments watching him as he sat there smiling contentedly. He was conscious only of a movement behind him as she snatched the bread knife from the table, and very conscious of pain as the knife went into his back.

Later on, in the police station, her face raddled with tears of guilt and self-hatred, and while Len struggled for life in the local hospital, all Marian could do was sob out over and over: "I knew he'd found another woman. I'd known it for months. He was so happy!"

The Stuff of Nightmares

Strangely enough I'd thought of Wicklow only the week before. I'd been reading a review in the *Times Literary Supplement* of a life of Hemingway, and reacted to the assertion: "All bullies are something else underneath, of course." I'd shaken my head. Wicklow wasn't, I said to myself: Wicklow was just bully through and through.

And now here he was on the other side of a smoky, beer-sodden Glasgow bar—the body even heavier, the face jowlier, the hair flecked with gray, but still unmistakably the Wicklow of my school days thirty years on. I shivered uncontrollably and buried my head in the *Literary Review*.

Perhaps it was not so strange that I'd thought of Wicklow so recently: I think he comes to my mind whenever instances of legalized cruelty come up—and heaven knows, that's often enough these days. It must have been 1960 when I saw him last, but that was two or three years after he had left Manorfield School. He used periodically to revisit the scene of his triumphs. The period of his greatest dominance was in the mid-fifties, notably the years 1956 to 1958, when he was a prefect. Then he was at his peak. He had always, I'm sure, tyrannized over boys smaller than himself, but as a prefect he had real power. One of my waking nightmares is a memory picture taken through my legs as I was bent over for punishment: it is of Wicklow running forward, cane raised. The memory is terrible not just for the pain that came after—the sharp, annihilating pain, repeated over and over—but especially for the expression of unbounded relish on his face. After the first stroke he always laughed—the laugh succeeding his victim's first cry of pain, telling him, as if he didn't know already, that any pleas for mercy would be so much wasted breath.

Wicklow wasn't just physically cruel: he had a nice line in psychological torments too. The most perilous position at Manorfield was that of a new boy whom Wicklow apparently befriended. The boy in question was always warned, but hope of avoiding the more dreadful manifestations of Wicklow's power by being favorite seemed to spring eternal. He could combine the psychological and the physical, as when he would overlook a minor offense with the chilling phrase: "I'll save it up." The end of this "saving" was always a beating of horrible ferocity.

You will say: "But this was the fifties. Things like that didn't happen then." Oh, but they did: they happened in some "good" schools, and they happened in many bad schools. Manorfield was a very bad school. I told my father what the place was like when I went home for the holidays, but he just shrugged and said it was part of the process of growing up, that I needed to be toughened up, that he wouldn't want people to say that any son of his was a ninny. I think his attitude was that *he'd* been through it in his time, so he didn't see why I shouldn't go through it in my turn. I think, even, that he rather enjoyed the thought. When, many years later, he begged me not to have him put in an old people's home I found it quite easy to harden my heart.

"Cardwell! If it isn't young Cardwell! Still got your nose buried in a book I see!"

His face was reflected, horribly distorted, in the wet barroom table, a twisted version of my nightmare picture. My heart sinking, my brain telling me over and over he could do nothing to me now, I looked up. There he was, standing over me as so often before: those rugby player's shoulders, the large hands now clutching a pint glass, the beer belly and above all the chilling smile. I nodded, casual, very cold, trying to disguise the fact that I still felt fear of him.

"Hello, Wicklow," I said.

He smiled, as if I'd just confirmed a suspicion.

"You'd seen me, hadn't you? Recognized me. And you didn't come over to say hello."

"Is there any reason why I should?"

"It would have been friendly. What are you having?"

I shook my head grimly and put my hand over my half-full wineglass.

"Wise man. I'm going to have to try to get rid of this." He patted his belly and went over to the bar. I sat there praying that was the end of the encounter, but knowing it was not. He brought his fresh pint over to my table and sat down. "That wasn't friendly, you know, Cardwell," he said, "seeing me over there on my own and shrinking into your—whatever it is." He waved his hand contemptuously at my periodical. "But then you always were a cagey little sod. What's the word? Introverted, that's it."

I tried to assert myself.

"Look, Wicklow, what is this about? I think I've made it pretty clear you're not welcome."

"You haven't been chummy," he admitted, with a mock air of forgiveness, "but I can't for the life of me see why not."

"If you're so thick that I have to spell it out, then I'll spell it out: you're not welcome because you're a sadist who made my school days a misery."

He laughed and spread out his hands.

"Good heavens, that was thirty years ago! What a time to nurse a grievance. Blame the system, blame the school."

"The system allowed it, you took advantage of it. You were the most appalling bully."

Wicklow smiled.

"I dispensed discipline."

"You did a whole lot more than that. And you enjoyed it."

"Of course I enjoyed it! It would have been a bloody silly waste of effort if I hadn't, wouldn't it?"

The frankness of the admission took me by surprise. He was beginning to fascinate more than repel me.

"You used to come back after you'd left—" I began.

"Oh boy, yes! I used to play with the First Fifteen when they just had friendlies. And then in the gym afterward. . . . I was in peak condition then. Though I say it myself, I was an artist. I had an agreement with the head boys who came after me. They used to save the hard cases for me to operate on. I used to look forward to those Saturdays. . . . Hated it when they came to an end."

Oh, the lovely English nostalgia for our school days!

"Yes, I remember my last two years were free of you," I said.

"An old aunt, last of her line, running a small manufacturing business, adopted me as her heir. I changed my name, took over the running of the business, moved up to Scotland." He sighed, his regret obviously genuine. "It was an offer I couldn't refuse, but there was some heart-searching, I can tell you."

"I can imagine you running a business," I said.

He laughed, that Wicklow laugh I remembered so well.

"You think I'm the sort of industrialist who lays off his workers just before Christmas, don't you?"

"Yes, Wicklow, I do."

"Not at all. Nothing so crude." His face twisted into the Wicklow smile. "But I do have a list of birthdays and wedding anniversaries."

"That figures," I said. "Are you married yourself?"

"I was, briefly. She couldn't stand the . . . pace."

"You really are an appalling man, aren't you?"

"I am what I am what I am. Blame the school."

"I don't respect people who are always trying to shift blame. You didn't have to use the system in the way you did."

"Good Lord, can you imagine anyone with my tastes *not*? And who's to say it wasn't the school, giving the older boys those powers, that nourished the tastes in me. You're not being logical, old man."

"I'm not feeling logical."

"Though, to be fair, a sadist will always find an outlet, one way or another. Look at the language politicians use when the mortgage rate goes up: 'hurt,' 'bite,' 'strong medicine.' I'm not very different to thousands of others. You just had a few bad times, that's all."

"You changed my whole character."

He shrugged.

"You look to me to be a perfectly normal man. Of a certain type."

I didn't rise to that last dig.

"You really have no shame, have you?"

"None whatsoever. I've had a good life on the whole. Shame should be felt when you haven't done what you could have done, even though you wanted to. I've usually been able to do what I've wanted to do. The only thing I've never done is murder anyone."

"You could murder my wife," I said.

We both laughed. A shared barroom joke that I despised

myself for having initiated. But as I drained my glass my hand shook at having given myself away to him. He put out his hand and took my glass.

"You'll have that refill now, won't you? Dry white? It would be."

By the time he returned from the bar I had got my breath back. The words had come out involuntarily because I was so preoccupied with what to do about Eileen. But I'd treated it as a joke, and he'd treated it as a joke.

"So what about you?" he said, settling his bulk down behind the table. "What do you do for a living?"

"Oh, nothing very exciting. I work for Nicolls, the publishers."

"Might have known it would be something bookish."

"Actually I'm on the production side. Oh, they give me a manuscript to advise on now and again, something in my field, or something on one of my hobbies. But mostly the job is practical and financial. I come up here once a fortnight because our printing works is here."

"Ah . . . But you live in London?"

"Yes. Or Bromley anyway. I commute, along with thousands of others."

"Nice house?"

"Nice enough. Bromley isn't exactly Olde Worlde. Still, it's big—bigger than we could afford if we were buying it now—and it's got plenty of ground. When you've been to boarding school you value privacy."

"That's right. Children? I should think you'd like children."

"No. My wife is . . . delicate."

"Ah, shame. But you like your job, do you? It's satisfying, I should think."

"Yes. Yes, it is that. I'd like to be on the editorial side—

that's where my interest lies. But I'm too useful on the production things—I'm up in the technology, very good at cost-
ing and so on. So I suppose that's where I'm stuck."

"And the . . . special interest: where does she work?"

"I'm sorry—"

"Come off it, Jeff—we're both men of the world." He
laughed hugely, and I hated the thought of being a man of
the world alongside him. "You're either having something on
the side, or there's a prospect in view."

Inevitably I produced my man-of-the-world credentials.

"Well, there is someone in Publicity. A lot younger than
me, but—well—she seems—"

"Interested. Good. Good for you! And hence your little
matrimonial problem." We both laughed. It was all a great
laugh. "But that shouldn't be a problem these days, should it?
I got rid of mine—well, strictly speaking, she flew the nest.
Why shouldn't you do the same, or persuade your wife to?"

"I've told you, she's delicate." My smile was bitter. "You've
no idea how delicate a delicate wife can be! She spends half
her life in bed. The fact is, her sanity's on a knife's edge."

He raised his eyebrows and laughed heartily again.

"Guilt. That's your problem, isn't it, Jeff? You can't do what you
want to because you would be consumed with guilt afterward."

And of course he was right.

"Yes. That is my problem."

"As I say, I've never felt that way. Perhaps I am the man to
help you with your . . . matrimonial problem."

He said it with a huge smile, and I laughed back at him.

"What do you propose? Some kind of *Strangers on a Train*
deal, where I do one for you in exchange?"

"Good Lord, no. If I wanted a murder done I wouldn't
choose a wimp like you to do it." I was still laughing, but

inside I cringed. What was it in me that wanted to live up to his horrible standards? "No," he went on, "what I was proposing was a personal service to you. You obviously feel some kind of bitterness—God knows why, after all these years—and I'm proposing to make it up to you."

"And achieve a personal ambition."

"And achieve a personal ambition. So make sure when you're up here again on—when will that be?—the seventeenth—"

"That's right. The seventeenth and eighteenth."

"—that you take someone out to dinner in the evening, make a late night of it, be at the works early in the morning and go home again in the usual way. When would that be?"

"I catch the midday train, get home a bit after six."

"There you are: problem solved."

This was all done with great grins, lots of laughter—as if we were still schoolboys, and schoolboys who liked each other. But inside my heart was beating fast.

"Joke over," I said. "I love my wife."

"Absolutely, old boy. All husbands do."

"There is no matrimonial problem."

"Quite. And you're getting younger every day, and the little thing in Publicity will wait forever. I get the picture. . . . Christ, I need a pee." He stood up, looming over me in the old way, looking down at me and smiling. "Of course I'd make it look like a robbery."

I sat there as he lumbered off to the lavatory, shouldering smaller drinkers aside. Half of me screamed that I had to escape from him, from his threatening presence and from the hideous memories he evoked. The other half told me to stay, to make sure it *had* been a joke, to get the message through to him that if he had been serious he'd better think again because *of course* I didn't want him to murder my wife. . . .

I sat, and sat, and sat. Wicklow did not return. His cruelty was as beautifully calculated as ever. After half an hour I went back to my hotel. It was an effort to behave normally as I collected my key at the desk. When I got to my room I ran into the bathroom and stood over the basin, retching, heaving, crying. As I lay on my bed afterward, staring at the ceiling, I remembered times at school when I had done exactly the same thing after sessions with Wicklow. Same old Wicklow, same old Cardwell. And a situation that nothing at Manorfield School had prepared me for.

With daylight things didn't seem quite so bad. On the long train trip home I reasoned that of course he had not been serious: it had just been one of Wicklow's "games"—those horrible playings with people that had been almost worse than the beatings. The whole thing had been the drama of an evening, something to enliven a chance encounter. True, the other half of me said that one way or another I'd given him all the information he needed, and something very deep down said I'd given him the information because I wanted him to have it, wanted him to do what he was engaging himself to do. But on the whole I had convinced myself by the time I returned home that it was all a nightmarish joke, nothing more. I could face Eileen with my usual cheerful patience. My usual wimpish, cringing eagerness to keep her happy.

Two days later I received his postcard. "Definitely interested in that business arrangement. Cheers, Chris."

I had forgotten his Christian name. Nobody thought of him as anything but Wicklow at school. A Christian name would have humanized him. The postcard was a view of

Durham, and it was posted in Berwick. It was addressed to my home—he must have got my address from the telephone directory, the only Cardwell in Bromley. I thought of getting on to Directory Inquiries and asking for a C. Wicklow in Berwick, but then I remembered he'd changed his name.

"Any letters, Jeff?"

Wicklow needn't have bothered to be enigmatic on the card. Eileen was never down to breakfast. Often she never came down at all. It was a red-letter day if she made it to the shops to get something for our dinner. Mostly we lived out of tins, and off prepared meals I bought at weekends and kept in the freezer.

"Only bills, darling."

Two days later, this time at work, I got another card: "Made all arrangements for our date? I have. Cheers, Chris." It was a picture of Dundee, posted in Bradford.

"I think I'd better take Peters and his wife out to dinner next time I go to Glasgow," I said to Taylor in Accounts.

"Why?" He flicked through his cards and peered at my entertainments account. "It's only nine months since you dined him last."

"It seems so unspontaneous to take him regularly every year in April. I think he's a bit discontented. He's a good man and we don't want to lose him."

"Oh, very well. But make it fifteen months before you take him out again."

Nicolls, you will have gathered, are not an open-handed firm. I rang Peters and made the arrangements. If he was surprised he was too polite to show it.

I hoped, through all this, that I was behaving normally. Susan, sadly, was the one it was most difficult to be with. She is a sweet girl, and very receptive to other people's moods, especially mine. The day before I was due to go up to Glasgow I received a last postcard: "It's as good as done. Best wishes. Chris."

It was a picture of Piccadilly Circus, and posted in SW1. I burned it, as I had burned the other two.

The things I do at the printing works in Glasgow are regular and standard, and I hope I did them this time in a regular and standard way. The dinner with Peters was more difficult. I tried not to be too hectic in my joviality, spun the meal out longer than usual by insisting we had brandies with our coffee. I think Peters was surprised when I suggested a nightcap in the bar of my hotel. It was by then half past ten, and the last flight from Glasgow to London had just gone—still, you couldn't be too careful. The Peterses agreed to "just a quick one," and when they left I named a wrong room number at Reception to make sure I was remembered. Not that it was necessary: I was a regular there, known and liked. I, who was hoping that at that very time Wicklow was murdering my wife. Was I hoping? Or merely planning in case he did? I cannot now disentangle my conflicting feelings.

The next day I went early down to breakfast, early off to the works, where Peters informed me that he and his wife had thoroughly enjoyed their evening. By eleven the various chores were done, and I had coffee with several of the management in the canteen. Then I took a taxi to the station.

On the train I relaxed my guard a little—relaxed my face muscles, allowed myself to frown, got myself a gin and tonic from the buffet. I pretended to read my *Guardian*, took out my papers and did one or two calculations of costs. But there was only one thing on my mind.

I crossed London, took the electric train to Bromley and walked home. It was by now well after six, and dark. There was no outside light on at my house, but then there often was not. Eileen forgot, or didn't bother. I let myself in, turned on the hall and outside lights, and shouted up the stairs:

"I'm home, darling."

There was no reply. There usually was a reply, unless we'd had a tiff. I left my case in the hall, went into the living room, where all was normal, then I went up the stairs. Heavily, reluctantly. There were no lights on, and everything was deathly still. Was I imagining it, or was there a smell—a terrible, insidious smell? I turned on the landing light, and then went to our bedroom door and turned on the light there.

The scene was terrible. She had known what was coming to her, but then I realized with a sickened shock that with Wicklow that would obviously have been part of the plan. The bed was terribly disturbed, and Eileen was lying across the foot of it in her nightdress, her throat cut and her blood everywhere. I screamed in genuine horror, ran halfway down the stairs, was pulled up by a fit of retching from which nothing came up, then I ran down the remainder of the stairs and picked up the phone in the hall. Clumsily, feverishly I dialed 999.

"Police! Quickly! My wife has been murdered! Please come! 25 Ravenscroft Avenue. Please! Please come!"

A patrol car was outside the house in five minutes, and in another minute or two a car with two detectives. I met them at the door, still ashen-faced and sobbing. They ran upstairs and I dragged myself up and stood on the landing, unable to look through the door, but bent against the wall, my forehead against the cool of it, sobbing, my stomach still heaving with disgust and fear.

"You've just got home, sir?" said the detective sergeant at the bedroom door. The three others came to join him there.

I nodded, swallowing.

"Yes. I've had two days in Glasgow, on business. She must have been killed last night while I was away."

"Last night, sir? She's still warm. The blood hasn't dried. I'd say she hasn't been dead half an hour."

"But that's impossible! He said—"

I raised my head and encountered the eyes of four policemen, looking at me with intense suspicion. I do not now know whether I heard, or simply seemed to hear, the familiar laugh of Wicklow from the garden.

BALMORALITY

I am going to write down a true account of the Merrivale busness without help from my secretary because I
know if it comes out I shall get blamed, especially by Mama,
who blames me for everything that goes wrong in her circle,
in Society in general—even, I sometimes think, in the country at large, as if I were somehow responsable for the national
debt, the troublesome Afgans, and the viragoes who advocate
votes for women. Nothing I say would influence Mama's
opinion, in fact nothing anybody says does, but perhaps an
account in my own hand, without the intervention of my
secretary, will convince posteraty that I was entirely blame-
less. Here is the whole truth of the matter.

The story begins in a corridor at Balmoral Castle, built in a
baronial but incomodious style by my revered father when I was
no more than a boy (but learning!). In Scotland the summer
nights are short, and the twilights almost seem to murge into the
first lights of dawn (especially for those of us who have
brought their own supplies to orgment the meager rations of
wines and spirits). I was, I must admit, in a pretty undignified
position for one of my standing. I was squeezed into an
alcove, perched on a sort of bench, shielded by heavy velvet curtains. Not a comfortable position for one of my gerth. I
would very much have prefered to stand, but I tried that and
found that my shoes pertruded under the bottom of the curtains.

So far I had seen nothing I did not expect to see. I had
seen Lord Lobway leave the comforts of his martial bed for

the delights of Mrs. Aberdovy's. I had seen Lady Wanstone
tiptoe along to comfort the loneliness of the Duke of Strath-
govern. I have corridor-tiptoed in my time, or been tiptoed
to, and I do not condem. I have nothing against adultary provided it is between consenting adults. Seducing a young girl is
the action of a cad, unless she is very insistant.

What I had not seen was the figure of that frightful fellow
John Brown. Now please do not misunderstand me here. I did
not for one moment expect to see the awful gillie going into my
Mama's bedroom. I do not suffer from the vulgar misappre-
hension about their relationship. In any case Mama's bedroom
is at least a quater of a mile away, otherwise I would not have
been hiding in the corridor! No, the door I was watching was that
of Lady Westchester, and the reason was twofold: if I could catch
John Brown out in a nocternal assignation with the lady, I
could take the story straight to Mama (I already had my sor-
rowful mein well prepared) and that would perhaps see the end
of his embarassing presence at her court; and secondly I have a
definate interest in Lady Westchester myself, and I object to
sharing her with a gillie. Her husband has been very willing to
turn a blind eye (and even, since he sleeps in the next room, a
deaf ear!) but I wonder whether he would be willing to do like-
wise for the repulsive Highlander? For when I heard Lady
Westchester, in intimate converse with her best friend, Mrs.
Aberdovy, say "He's so deliciously ordinary!" that, I concluded,
was who she was talking about. I had seen her fluttering her eye-
lids at him when he helped her to horse. And which of the other
servants mix with Mama's guests on that level of familiarity (or
impurtenance)? When she begged me not to trouble her that
night (I had not noticed it was any trouble) then I concluded that
her assignation was with one infinately lower than myself.

Dinner had been oxtail soup, sole, foie gras, turbot, snipe, crown of beef, game pie, steamed pudding, and one or two other trifles I had just picked at, but dinner was hours and hours ago. I was just beginning to feel hungry when I heard the sound of a door opening. I peered through the heavy folds of velvet. It was not Lady Westchester's door. I was about to withdraw into my alcove when I saw a scene in the open doorway that gave me furiously to think. The door was Colonel Merrivale's, and coming out was a little bounder called Laurie Lamont, whose presence at Balmoral I found it difficult to account for. But what made my heart skip a beat was that I could see clearly that Merrivale was withdrawing his hand from the inside of his jacket, while Laurie Lamont's hand was withdrawing from the pocket of his trousers.

Not an hour before Merrivale had been winning quite heavily off me and other gentlemen at poker.

Lamont scuttled off down the corridor and away to his room in some obscure corner of my Papa's Gothick pile, and I remained considering the scene I had just witnessed and hoping that the gastly gillie would make his appearance soon. I had waited no more than a few minutes when I heard footsteps. Looking out I saw that it was my own man! I shrank back, but the footsteps stopped beside my alcove.

"I would advise Your Royal Highness not to remain here any longer."

Well! He had barely paused, spoke in a low voice, and then continued on down the corridor. After thinking things over for a few minutes I emerged rather nonchalently and returned to my suite of rooms. Where my man awaited me.

"How did you know I was there?" I demanded.

"I am afraid, sir, there was a certain swelling which disturbed the hang of the curtain."

He has a clever way of putting things, my man. He meant

there was a bulge. He is fair, tall, with an air that is almost
gentlemanly and an expression that I have heard described as
quizicle.

"Where had you come from anyway?" I asked.

"I was myself watching from another alcove," he replied. I
looked with distast at his discusting slimness. "I too had had
my suspicions roused in the course of cards this evening."

I did not enlighten him as to which door I had in fact been
keeping an eye on, or give any indication that the scene in the
doorway had come as a complete bomshell to me. As he
releived me of my clothes I let him continue.

"You remember, sir, that you summoned me to prepare
some of the herbal mixture that you get such releif from, after
too many cigars?"

"Shouldn't be getting short of breath these days," I complained. "I've cut down to just one before breakfast, and the
odd cigarette."

"I rather fear that without noticing you have increased
your consumption *after* breakfast, sir," he said. I allow my
man great lattitude. He is invaluable in all sorts of little
arrangements. "Anyway, the fact was I was in the card room
for some time, during which Colonel Merrivale was winning
quite heavily."

"Too damned heavily. I'm well out of pocket."

"Exactly, sir. And I noticed this Mr. Lamont. He was deep
in converse with the Countess of Berkhampstead. She was
telling him about her various ailments, and was so
engrossed—predictably so, if I may venture to say it—that
she was noticing nothing about him. They were by a mirror.
By testing I realized he could see the cards of two of the other
players. And I got the idea that he was making suttle signs to
Colonel Merrivale."

"The damned rotters!" I exploded. "At Balmoral too! Windsor would be another matter, but Balmoral! I know Merrivale. He's brother to one of the Queen's Scottish equerries. Who is this Lamont fellow?"

"I have made inquiries about that, sir—talked to his man. He is active in civic affairs in Edinburgh, it seems. Has been pressing the case for a fitting monument in the city to the late Prince Consort. He has been agitating in the City Council and the newspapers for an Opera House, to be called the Albert Theatre."

"It will never happen. The good burgers of Edinburgh are far too mean."

"It may be, sir, that he doesn't expect it to happen, and that that is not the point. He has, after all, been invited to Balmoral. . . ."

I told you he was sharp. I took his point at once.

"True. Mingling with those very much above his station."

"Quite, sir."

"Mama is too gulable. It's too much that people get invited here at the drop of the word 'Albert.' "

"I suspect it has been noted, sir, that the name is a sort of Open Sessamy."

"The bounders have to be exposed."

"Quite so, sir. But how?"

"I can charge him publicly with what I saw."

"Hardly conclusive, sir. And I see a difficulty: you were playing poker, for money, at Balmoral, sir."

He was his usual impurturbable self, but I huffed and puffed a bit, though nothing like as much as Mama would have huffed and puffed if she knew we had been playing poker for high stakes in what is vertually my late Papa's second morsauleum.

"Ah yes, well . . ." I said finally. "Might be a bit awkward. Though when I think how the Queen goes on about the company I keep . . ."

"Perhaps we should sleep on it, sir. By morning we may have thought of something."

"Nothing to do but think," I muttered, as he pulled my nightshirt over my head. I leapt between the sheets, burning my leg on the stone hot water bottle. "I'm not used to sleeping alone. Alix would have been better than nothing."

For my dear wife has no love of Balmoral, and generally siezes the time of our annual visit for a trip to see her relatives. I make no objection. If her relatives had been German Mama would probably find her visits to them admirably fillial, but as they are Danish she says she is being selfish.

Well, I spent a lonely night warmed only by hot water bottles, but I can't say that in the morning I had come up with any great plan. All I could think of was whether John Brown was in with Lady Westchester, and what they were likely to be doing. Mind you, I don't think my man expected me to come up with anything. When he said we he meant I. He's got rather a good opinion of himself.

"Well, sir," he said next morning, as he shaved the bits of my face that needed shaving, "it's a beuatiful day, and apparently the vote is for a croquy competition."

"Damned boring game," I commented. "Bonking balls through hoops."

"But you do play, sir."

"Oh, I can bonk with the best of them."

"Because I thought just possibly something might be made of it."

And he wisked off the towels just like the johnnie in the opera, and confided in me his thoughts.

The Arbroath smokies served at Balmoral are, I have to admit, unparalleled, and the kedgeree not to be despised. The sausages, bacon, and black pudding are inferior to what we have at Marlborough House, but the beefsteaks can be admirable. I breakfasted alone. If I take a small table and look Royal everybody knows I am brooding on affairs of state and I am not disturbed. When I had eaten my fill I lit my second cigar of the day and strolled out on to the sun-drenched lawns. It did not even destroy my good humor to see John Brown setting up the hoops and pegs and three seperate croquy lawns. Somehow I knew things were going to go according to plan.

Lord John Willoughby had been recruited to further the plot. Lord John is in fact alergic to croquy, but he was a fellow loser of the night before, and he was to be used as an apparently casual bystander. He had been approached by a deputation consisting of my man, and he had joyfully gone along with the idea. Those villians Merrivale and Lamont had been organized by Willoughby into opposing teams, and when I strolled up to Merrivale and said "Give me my revenge for last night, eh?" Lord Rishton willingly dropped out of the game and transferred to another team, which left me partnering the loathsome Lamont, with Merrivale's partner the delectible Lady Frances Bourne, whose only fault is her unshakable faithfulness to a damned dull husband. Still, if I couldn't partner her in any other sort of games, croquy it would have to be.

Willoughby, I'll say this for him, has a sense of humor. He arranged it so he stood on the sidelines of our game talking to Lady Berkhampstead. He was, to all intents and purposes, totally absorbed in her twinges of this and aggonising attacks of that. I let the game proceed until I was well-poised to shoot my red ball through the fourth hoop and Lamont was rather poorly placed for getting his yellow ball through the third.

Then, as he was standing beside his ball shielding it from the gaze of spectators, I gave the sign and both Willoughby and I stepped forward.

"That man moved his ball."

Laurie Lamont looked astonished, as well he might.

"I haven't touched my ball, sir. It's not my turn."

"I'll have no partner of mine cheating," I said.

"I saw him," said Willoughby, coming up. "He shifted his ball to a better position for his next shot."

"And where there's cheating, there's money on the game," I said menacingly. "I wouldn't mind bet—I strongly suspect that they've got a wager on this."

I looked meaningfully at Lamont, then equally meaningfully at Merrivale. I wanted both of them to understand *exactly* what piece of cheating was in question.

"And since no one would suspect Lady Frances of betting, I think we can take it that you, Merrivale, are the other culprit. Betting on a game of croquy in the grounds of the Queen's Scottish home! And cheating! You probably even have the wager on you, I'll be bound."

I knew they did. Lamont had his on him because he's one of those tradesmen chappies who won't leave loose money in their rooms even when they're guests of their Sovereign. Merrivale had his on him because his man had been persuaded by mine to slip it into the inside pocket of his jacket that morning.

"I absolutely protest, sir," he now spluttered. "I have no money on me!"

He opened his jacket, and pertruding from the pocket was an envelope. I extracted it and counted the money.

"One hundred and fifteen pounds. And no doubt you too have a hundred and fifteen?" Lamont squermed and kept his jacket tight-buttoned. I held out my hand and with aggonized reluctance he took out the money. "Two hundred and thirty pounds. Well, well, well!"

It was the sum Merrivale had won the night before, shared equally with his accomplice. I pocketed it.

By now there were several bystanders, all curious to know what was going on. Lady Berkhampstead, interrupted midtwinge, was loudly demanding to be told what was happening. I pointed to the Castle.

"Betting at Balmoral. I never thought to see the day. You, sir"—I turned to Merrivale—"I would have expected to know better. You, sir"—turning to Lamont—"I had no expectations of. I count on hearing that you have both left the Castle before nightfall."

There was a moment's pause. Merrivale spluttered, then the pair of them slunk in the direction of the Castle, their tails almost visably between their legs. I walked over in high good humor to watch one of the other games.

"Just a little contratems," I said airily. "Regard our game as scratched."

That evening, when my man was poking and prodding me into my evening wear to make me presentable for the dreary horrors of a Balmoral dinner, he said:

"Colonel Merrivale's young daughter has been taken ill, and Mr. Lamont's mother. Quite a coincidence, sir."

I grunted my satisfaction, and in an interval of prodding said: "That'll teach the Queen not to invite just any little squert who happens to suck up to her on the subject of Papa. I wonder if I should rub it in that she ought to be more careful who she invites?" I saw an expression pass over his face. I am very quick on the uptake. "Well, perhaps not. Perhaps I may just write an account of the whole busness for posterity."

"That should make fasinating reading, sir."

My mind going back to the start of the busness and my concealment in the alcove, I said:

"Lady Westchester has intimated that I would be welcome tonight. Don't know that I shall take up the offer. Damned unpleasant not knowing who I'm sharing her with."

"I happen to know, sir, that the reason Lady Westchester was . . . unavailable last night was because her husband especially requested the favor of a night with her. The sort of ladies his lordship habitually consorts with are in particularly short supply in the Balmoral area."

"Really?" I said, rather pleased. But then I pondered. "That doesn't explain the other thing, though."

"Other thing, sir?"

"I heard her say of some man that he was 'delicously ordinary.' I'm damned sure she was talking about John Brown."

There came over my man's face that smile that people call quizicle.

"Oh that, sir. Is that what you suspected? Her ladyship has been heard to say that to several people. I think she intends the remark to be paradoxicle."

"To be what?"

"A paradox, sir, is something that is apparently abserd or impossible, but turns out to be true. Her ladyship was not referring to John Brown, sir."

"Oh?"

"She was referring to you."

For a moment he took my breath away. When the idea got through to me I felt immensely flattered.

"Well, I say, you know, that really is rather a complement, don't you think? I mean, here I am, with all my advantages, rather marked off by my birth, set apart all my life for a special task, and yet I manage to keep the common touch to such an extent that she can say that about me. I feel quite touched. She's right. I am ordinary. No one would call the Russian Emperor ordinary, would they? Or the Kaiser? She really has me summed up very well."

"I'm glad Your Royal Highness sees it that way."

"I do. I'm obliged to you for clearing up the misunderstanding. In fact I'm obliged to you for giving the other matter such a satisfactory outcome too."

I felt about my person for something with which to show my appreciation of his very special services. It is one of the drawbacks of being royal that one has very little use for ready money, so one very seldom has any on one. Fortunately I have always found that people feel just as well rewarded by a sincere expression of Royal gratitude. I clapped my man on the shoulder.

"Thank you, Lovesey," I said.

LIVING WITH JIMMY

When I think about my mother in those years when I was growing up, the image that comes into my mind is an ashtray—a large, shiny blue one, piled high—the neat brown filter tips nestling in the untidy rubble of gray ash. Eventually, when no more could be got into it, the ashtray would be tipped into the rubbish bin under the sink, but never washed. Then the process of filling it would begin over again. It stays in my mind, this ashtray, a still life in blue, brown and gray— an image of my mother's boredom: I bored her, her life with me bored her, she bored herself. You can imagine how interesting my life was.

Meanness is unfortunately not one of my father's many faults. If he had been meaner then perhaps my mother would have been forced to get a job, find someone to mind me after school and in the holidays, see new people, perhaps even make friends. That way she might have met someone or done something interesting which we could have talked about when I came home from school. But, as it was, the alimony or maintenance money (she never said what it was, just calling it "my money" when the check came in the post) arrived regularly, and was apparently generous. We never wanted for anything. And meanwhile my mother did a bit of cooking, a bit of housework, a bit of shopping and went quietly mad with boredom, of which the filter tips in the ashtray were a symptom and a symbol. I understand this very well now, at sixteen, but I think I understood it even then, though I would not have been able to find words for it. Naturally I worried more about the dismal quality of my own life.

About twice a year my father came to take me out. This enabled us to get to know each other better: he to find out that I was a thoroughly uninteresting little girl, I to find out that he was a rather nasty man. I, of course, hid my more interesting thoughts from him (one would hardly tell them to someone one saw twice a year), while he could not hide his essential qualities from me. The noise of his car starting up to drive him away always sounded in my ears like a sigh of relief.

Meanwhile on those days my mother had been loafing around the house, working up a good, acrid fug. She was never inventive enough to think up anything interesting or exciting to do while I was out of the way. She was what the tabloids would call an accident waiting to happen—or a bomb waiting to be exploded. Or a victim waiting to be murdered.

I was with her when she met Jimmy Wildman. It was holiday time, summer, so inevitably I was with her. There were clothes to buy for me for the start of the new school term, and my mother said she was tired of the "filthy" local shops (she had a very limited vocabulary, which put me to shame on the rare occasions when she came to school functions). So we had driven in the little Allegro into Barstow, where we had found new shoes and a new coat for me, and done a bit of desultory shopping for her too. She was not one of those compulsive shoppers—like everything else, it soon became a bore. It was a hot day, and my mother then declared that she felt like a drink—unusually for her, for drink was not one of her problems. We found a pub with would-be rustic wooden tables and benches outside, and my mother went into the bar and got an orange squash for me, and gin and tonic for her.

Whether Jimmy Wildman sat down at the next table with

a formed intention of picking her up, I don't know. There were other, more desirable women there that morning, even if you were attracted by the smell of nicotine, and they were unencumbered with a child in attendance. I think I noticed him before my mother did, because I was sitting facing him and I noticed things because the bench was uncomfortable, like all benches.

He was wearing jeans and a loose denim jacket over an ill-fitting T-shirt. He was big, but I thought it was the bigness of fat as much as of muscle (I was thirteen then, you see, and beginning to notice young males and how they looked). His hands were rough, and a dark stubble sprouted on his chin and cheeks. His eyes were bloodshot, his skin white, his hair long and greasy. He was very unattractive.

My mother was rummaging in her handbag searching for a new packet of cigarettes and looking rather flushed.

"I'm getting hotter and hotter, not cooling down," she muttered.

"Perhaps you shouldn't be drinking gin and tonic," I said, looking around. "Everyone else seems to be drinking beer and lager and stuff like that."

She looked around.

"Do you know, I think you're right," she said in a surprised voice, as if I had never said anything sensible in my life before. She pushed the half-finished drink away from her and marched back to the bar, cigarette hanging from her mouth.

It was that, the pushing away of the gin and tonic, that told Jimmy Wildman that my mother had money. Not necessarily loads of money, but the sort of money that means you're not always worrying about money. Enough.

I saw it then, you see, as a matter of money. I can see now that there were other things. Sex, for example. Jimmy was recently out of jail, he was desperate for a woman, and if there were many more attractive women than my mother around, it was also true that they were women Jimmy was not likely to get to bed unless he took a lot of trouble with himself, which would certainly be unlike Jimmy. My mother, like her money, was enough.

"Got a light?"

He took no trouble, you notice, even with his opening gambit.

Within a couple of minutes he was at our table, drinking the remains of my mother's gin and tonic as if he were doing it a favor, and asking about the neighborhood ("wondered whether it would be worthwhile slinging my hook here"). I don't remember much about the conversation, which was not memorable, only that before we left my mother said:

"There's a ladies' lav over there, Jennifer. Go and use it before we get in the car."

"I don't want to go."

"Do as I say. You'll only grizzle about wanting to go when we're on the road, you know you will."

I had never in my life grizzled in the car about wanting to go to the lavatory. This habit of putting me down in public was one that annoyed me very much. I knew then that we had not seen the last of Jimmy. I saw it for certain in the knowing manner with which they said good-bye.

He moved in two nights later. He arrived in the evening in a battered old car with one month to run of an MOT that must have been obtained sight unseen. All his belongings, nothing much, were in the back of it. It was in the course of the evening that he told us he was just out of jail. He showed no embarrassment about it. When my mother asked what for he said with a shrug: "Breaking and entering." So unembarrassed was he that I thought he was telling the truth, though in fact he was not. He stayed the night as—shocked but fascinated—I had known he would.

I saw him next morning, on his way to the bathroom-lavatory, quite naked. It was the first time I had seen a grown man naked, and I can't say it interested me particularly. I was on my way downstairs, and I thought it would be impolite to take any particular notice. What I did notice, though, was that his sloppy clothes had misled me: there was a lot more muscle than fat. I should have guessed this. You do not get overfed in prison.

When I asked my mother she said that he'd be stopping for a bit.

"Do you know what you're doing?" I asked.

"I've been alone for so long," she said, shrugging. This was no grand passion, I concluded. But I said:

"I don't like it."

"I'll see you don't come to any harm," she said.

That possibility hadn't even occurred to me.

And so Jimmy Wildman settled down with us. His personal habits were far from nice. He ate hunched over his plate, shoveling the food in in a hit-and-miss fashion. He spent much of the day in front of the television, watching cartoons for preference. His personal hygiene was appalling, but I never heard my mother try to do anything about this.

I began to think that Jimmy Wildman was not the sort of man a young girl ought to have around her in her impressionable years.

He used to go to pubs most evenings. Sometimes my mother would go with him; sometimes—if they were driving out somewhere, and there was little danger of my meeting anyone from school, or their parents, and being embarrassed—I would go too. On nice evenings we would sit outside the pub, and sometimes Jimmy would get quite jolly, and a group would gather around him, laughing. He would introduce himself to strangers by banging his chest and saying, "Me Wild Man."

I could have died, he was so common.

One of my father's reluctant and infrequent visits was promised for early October. One day on the stairs I happened to overhear my mother and Jimmy in the sitting room.

"Jennifer's dad's coming on Saturday. Best make yourself scarce."

"Why the hell should I? Are you supposed to live like a bloody nun, when he upped and left you?"

"He's the goose that lays the golden eggs. We don't want him making any trouble about Jennifer."

There was a pause and then Jimmy said: "I'll take off for the day."

I took that as a useful hint: the money coming in was for me, so it could be used to put pressure on my mother. On Saturday, when my father came to fetch me, he said he thought we'd go to the zoo. I made no objections, though I disapprove on principle of keeping animals in captivity. I thought it would be a good place to talk, so an hour or two later, when we were looking at a bored grizzly bear, and it was looking back at us boring each other, I said:

"Mummy's got a new boyfriend."

"Has she now?"

I looked to see whether he was anticipating saving money, but my father has a very noncommittal face, due to his not having very much in the way of interests or opinions.

"He's yucky. He's hulking and very working-class, and he's been in jail."

"Well, I wouldn't want to say anything against your

mother," he said, preparing to, "but she never had much taste, and she can hardly pick and choose at her time of life."

Where, I wondered but did not say, did that leave him?

"He's got disgusting habits, and he doesn't even keep himself clean. He smells!"

"Hmmm." (I could have been talking about the family dog.)

"It's not very nice for me, growing up with someone like that around."

"No, it can't be. But I don't see what I can do. You can't come and live with me."

"I didn't mean that."

"And your mother is a free agent."

"There's the money you send her."

"The money is for you. And it doesn't sound as if the boyfriend is in the high income bracket."

Well, at least that confirmed my suspicion, but it didn't get me much further forward. When he let me out of the car outside the semi I called home, he said:

"Keep me posted about your mother's boyfriend."

Thank you for your concern, I muttered to myself as I went through the gate and up the path to the door.

Jimmy kept away until late that evening. When he came back he was flushed with drink and was carrying a four-can pack of Export lager. I had noticed that my mother never seemed to give him any money for himself, but that after he'd been out in the evenings on his own he usually had cash to spare for the next day or two. I turned over in my mind what to make of this observation, but came to no conclusion. Since he always used the car—our car—I was unable to follow him to see what he was doing.

One day when I was talking to the headmistress about what I was to take next year I suddenly told her about him. It came out almost without my intending it.

"There's a man living in our house now. My mum's boy-friend. He's hulking and common—he just sits around all day eating and watching telly."

"Oh dear," said Miss Forster, interested.

"I think he could be violent."

"Has there been any violence toward you or your mother?"

"Not toward me. I don't think there has yet against Mother, but I'm not sure. I'm afraid of him. He's not the sort of person should be around a growing girl."

"No, I can see that. . . . But I'm not sure that there's anything I can do."

She did, I later learned, ring my mother and make an appointment "to talk over Jennifer's future." My mother never turned up. Not that one could necessarily blame that on Jimmy. In the days before she met him she probably wouldn't have turned up for such a meeting either.

"I wish you'd get rid of Jimmy," I said to my mother, a week or so after that. "I don't like the way he keeps eyeing me. It's disgusting."

"Eyeing you?"

"Yes—you know, sexually."

"You don't know anything about it."

"Yes, I do. I'm going to lock my door."

"Go ahead. I know you're making it up, because I know Jimmy doesn't fancy young girls. He fancies older women, thank God. I see who he eyes off when we're out together."

She flounced out of the kitchen, bumping into the open door. She was very clumsy, my mother. I thought: Well, that was another approach that didn't work. She was quite right. The women Jimmy looked at when we were out at pubs and places were all plump, maternal types. Pathetic I called it.

The next day the knock my mother had taken by bumping

into the door had come up into a nasty blue bruise. I was pleased. I was standing at the bus stop on my way to school when Mrs. Horrocks from next door came past.

"Hello, Jennifer. How's your mother? I haven't seen her for ages."

"She's all right. . . . Well, not really. She's got this nasty bruise."

"A bruise? How did she get that?"

"You know. . . . That man . . ."

"Man? The one that's stopping with you?"

"Her boyfriend."

"Well! I thought he was a cousin or nephew or something!"

I stared at the ground, and Mrs. Horrocks went on her way, shaking her head. I congratulated myself that I had not even told her a lie, though I was quite willing to if necessary. I did later in the day when I went specially to see Miss Forster and tell her. She also shook her head.

"If only your mother had come to see me, dear. We could have talked it over. Perhaps *I* should go and pay a call on *her*."

She did, later that day. My mother called her an interfering old bag when I got home that afternoon, and Miss Forster told me the next day that my mother had insisted that she collided with a door.

"Such a silly story. As if she just couldn't be bothered to make up a better one. I'm beginning to be quite worried about you." She added: "If you should ever need a home, Jenny dear, you can always rely on me."

The next thing that happened was that the police came for Jimmy. They came on a Saturday when he was deeply absorbed in the Flintstones or Corky the Cat, and after a bit of talk in the living room they took him away. I suppose he was "helping the police with their inquiries," which I always thought was a silly phrase: I couldn't see Jimmy as a Dr. Watson. My mother said: "The bloody police. They always pick on past offenders." I shrugged and said: "Seems a sensible place to start." She got very ropey.

The annoying thing was that by late afternoon Jimmy was back and wanting to know what had happened to Corky the Cat. The police had hoped to pin a pilfering raid in Kettlesham on him, but the night it had occurred he had been with my mother in Barstow, at the pub where they had met, and where they were by now fairly well known. Right man, wrong job. I conceived a low opinion of the local police which I have had no reason to alter since.

I need hardly say that the arrival of the policemen, and their going off with Jimmy, had been observed by the whole neighborhood, most of them cleaning their cars or clearing up leaves on their front lawns at the time. I began to be showered with looks of pity when they passed me in the street.

It was now approaching Christmas. My mother had had no more accidents that showed, unfortunately: she was clumsy but not absolutely incapable physically. The thought of Christmas with Jimmy, and the endless diet of television pap aimed at people with a mental age of ten, was not pleasant. I said:

"I think we should go away for Christmas."

It was typical of my mother that she had never thought of the idea of going away for Christmas for herself, and typical too that once it came up it appealed to her immensely: no fuss of cooking, decorating the house, stocking up with goodies. The burden reduced, in fact, to buying something for me (I always told her what I wanted), and this year something for Jimmy (almost anything in the clothes line would be acceptable, since his wardrobe was an Adidas bag). My mother said, uncertainly:

"But where do you *go*, if you go away for Christmas? What do people *do?*"

"They go to hotels. There's one in the paper tonight offering a three-day Christmas away-break, at Seccombe."

"It would be *nice.*"

"A hundred and fifty pounds in all, children at half price."

"I suppose I could manage that."

"Jimmy would need some new clothes," I pointed out.

"Oh, that's all right. I was thinking of kitting him out for Christmas anyway."

Jimmy did not look particularly gratified or even interested, and he didn't say what he was thinking of getting her: it depended, presumably, on what he could pick up.

"I could ring them and book," I said.

I have a very adult voice, and an excellent vocabulary. It was always best to do things like that myself, since if I left it to Mother it would probably not get done. After some thought I booked us in as Mr. and Mrs. Wildman and Jennifer Burton (child). Child of a previous marriage, I impressed on my mother.

"I don't know why I should lie about being married to Jimmy," she complained. "Nobody cares these days."

"They would care at a hotel in Seccombe," I said, and added nastily: "It looks bad enough as it is."

That, as it turned out, was putting it mildly. The clientele at the Devonshire Arms at Seccombe were fiftyish or over, twinset and pearls if they were women, tweeds and pipes if they were men. Middle-aged women with toy boys were not part of their mental world. They gave the impression that they had spent their lives choking off unwanted familiarities, and it seemed as if the whole point for them of celebrating Christmas in a hotel was to show that they knew how to Keep Themselves to Themselves. Jimmy in a suit and tie only meant that the temperature was nine below instead of ten below. Any communication there was occurred between the men in the bars, where it was established that the "marriage" of Jimmy and my mother was recent, and I was not his child. It was immediately assumed I was an illegitimate product of my mother's gay youth, and I was "poor-deared" by the kindlier of the women there, and pointedly ignored by the beastlier. Any attempts at jollity at our table (and Jimmy only tried two or three times) lowered the temperature in the room still further.

It didn't worry my mother. To care what other people think of you, you have first to notice. She ate the food, which was conventional but good, drank the odd glass of wine, leaving the rest of the bottle to Jimmy, and generally seemed to have quite a satisfactory time of it. They spent a lot of time in bed, but as there was television in each room they could well have been watching *The Sound of Music*.

I had announced from the beginning that I wanted to go to Hatherton Towers. That is the point about Seccombe. It is a very snooty little town, but the nearest stately home has been turned into an enormous leisure park and funfair—a sort of Disneyland without the class. If my mother had known anything about me at all she would have found it surprising that I should want to go anywhere as childish and vulgar as Hatherton Towers, but she didn't and when I asked she just nodded. I needn't have bothered insisting, in fact: Jimmy was determined to go anyway. It was aimed at his mental age.

We went on Boxing Day. It had been closed in the run-up to Christmas and on The Day itself, but on Boxing Day families start shaking themselves out of their overfed torpor and getting out and about. Normal families, I mean. My mother swore about the steep admission charges, but the man at the ticket office explained that the price covered all the amusements and sideshows. "The little girl will have a whale of a time," he said. I shot him a glance that should have shriveled him, but he'd already gone on to smarming over the next family.

Well, Hatherton Towers had all the forced jollity and unforced vulgarity that I had expected, but I made myself go on a few things, and Jimmy capered around like a five-year-old, and would have gone on everything if there'd been time. I bided my time for an hour or so, until I saw what I wanted, and when I saw it I bided my time until the crowd moved in another direction, then I pointed.

"I want to go on that."

That was a super-high slide, snaking its way down round a central tower.

"Great!" said Jimmy, rubbing his hands and dancing toward it.

"You go," said my mother. "There's no bloody lift. I'm not climbing that ladder."

"Come on," I said, pulling her. "I'm not going up there with him on my own."

Grumbling, cursing, she started up.

"Come *on*," shouted Jimmy down to us. "It's going to be a great slide down! You've no energy!"

"Too bloody right!" shouted my mother back. "I'm thirty-eight. I grew out of this sort of lark when I was fifteen."

The sound of their voices penetrated back to the odd family on the ground. It was the best I could do. I'd given up hope of organizing a public row. Their temperaments were too similar. The word "sluggardly" would describe it best.

Jimmy was already at the top when we reached it. There was a waist-high fence which offered adequate protection for children. Jimmy was rubbing his hands at the top of the chute. My mother looked over the railings. "Christ Almighty!"

she said (she was inclined to blaspheme). "All this bloody way up just to go down again."

A second later she was on the ground, spread-eagled out, with a crowd gathering round her. A second or two later Jimmy arrived at the bottom of the chute to find her already dead. I meditated whether to go down on the slide, which was obviously the quickest way, but it would have given the impression of heartlessness, so I began screaming instead.

I must say I never expected Jimmy to be accused of murder. I had underestimated forensic science. My mother had fallen plumb downwards on her face, and there were marks on her back that could only have been caused by a hefty shove. The police had assumed it was an accident, but once the report came through they had no hesitation in arresting him, and the case was so straightforward that it was quite swiftly brought to trial. I gave evidence that they'd had a bit of an argument on the way up, and implied that this was par for the course. I said I'd seen nothing on the top platform because I'd been looking over the railings on the other side.

The Defense, a pushy young man supplied on Legal Aid, went in all directions in his unconvincing attempts to save Jimmy. I was not in court, of course, but I had all the gen passed on to me by school friends. (Miss Forster tried to protect me by keeping the newspapers from me—I'd asked to go to her as soon as I knew my mother was dead—but, of course, in a school everything gets out.) First the Defense tried to shake the forensic evidence, but the expert said there was no way it could have been an accident. Then they tried to argue that Jimmy had found an easy berth, and there was no way he was going to ruin it. The young man pointed out that he was a criminal of the most petty: he had had two periods of probation, one involving community work (unsatisfactorily performed), and one three-month jail sentence, all for shop-lifting and petty pilfering (so much for breaking and enter-ing—Jimmy couldn't have summoned up the nerve to break and enter to save his life). Defense pointed out that he had never been involved in violence, and the police had to agree with this. The police, in fact, seemed quite to like Jimmy, but they pointed out that he was an immature individual, was involved in a long-term relationship for the first time and had acted on the spur of the moment. That was why they were willing to reduce the charge to manslaughter.

Defense then turned, gingerly, to me. I was young, and resented my mother's new affair, and perhaps was afraid of her lover. Prosecuting Counsel vigorously objected. If the emotions were felt at all, they would not have been a motive for murdering the mother, but for murdering the lover. (Did they really think I was such a dumb cluck as to commit a murder for which I would be the most likely suspect?) The forensic expert was recalled and expressed the view that it was most unlikely that a girl of thirteen would have the necessary strength to inflict the blow that had sent my mother over the parapet (so much for experts).

I must say I did wonder whether the police would do tests on the slide—whether they would find out that Jimmy could not have pushed my mother over and then arrived at the bot-tom a second or two later. But then, people's memories are not reliable where time is concerned, particularly at moments of crisis. And as I said, the local police are not all that bright.

So Jimmy was found guilty of manslaughter and sentenced to nine years. With remission for good conduct (and I can't see him having the nerve for anything else) he should be out in three or four years. I sometimes worry about this, but, after all, by then I will be at university, and what could he do if he found out where I was beyond accuse me? I just don't see him having the energy.

On the whole, living with Miss Forster has worked out very well. When my father comes on his twice-yearly visits his face has an expression of relief on it, that someone could be found to take me on and relieve him of the responsibility. Miss Forster fusses a lot, is much too protective, but after my childhood this makes a nice change. It's true that recently there have been signs of something else that I certainly don't like—trying to get too close to me, touching me unnecessarily, that sort of thing. There's a teacher at school who's taken a big interest in me since my mother's death. Her family is grown up, so I could go and live with her. I wouldn't have to go to extremes with Miss Forster—just a few allegations to the police or the social worker who visits now and then would do the trick. I wouldn't think of doing anything more drastic. It would be unfortunate if people began to associate me in their minds with violent death.

IF LOOKS COULD KILL

*W*hen Sam and I married everybody said it was a mésalliance. On his part, of course. *His* people stood around eyeing off *my* people at the reception, and they hardly bothered to hide their scorn. My people were not very numerous. There was my mother and Auntie Florrie, both there for the booze. There was my best friend Val and a few girls from work who were hardly more than "friends for the day." And that was about it. I have always preferred to go through life unencumbered.

His people, Sam's, ranged from the comfortably off to the discreetly rich. They were Jewish, though few of them were Orthodox, as over the years they had Englished themselves determinedly. The men wore the right suits for a wedding, the women wore the right dresses and everyone wore the right expression—that of trying to put the best face on a disaster.

"They're wearing their *Titanic* expressions," I said to Val.

"Snotty-nosed bunch," she said. "What have they to sneer at?"

"I'm not their class, I'm not their race, and I'm not their religion," I pointed out.

That was it, really. The whole reception consisted of my people trying to get the lion's share of the drinks and eats, and his people making it clear that in marrying me Sam Kopinski had let down not only his family but his whole world.

"We must hope for the best," his sister said to me as a hired caterer poured her a second glass of champagne. "Sometimes a marriage of opposites turns out surprisingly well."

"We are rather the long and short of it," I said, deliberately misunderstanding. "Anyway, we've given it a good trial, so we're pretty sure we'll be able to make a go of it."

The look she gave me made it clear that that was not the sort of thing that was said at weddings in Kopinski circles.

Physically, as I say, we made a pretty funny picture walking down the aisle. Sam was about five foot two, with a figure that could best be described as squat. He looked like a frog who's been in the hands of a circus trainer. His features were—unlike most of his family's—splendidly Jewish, and he rejoiced in it. "Why try to look what you're not?" he used to ask. "If I tried to look Eton and Oxford I wouldn't succeed, and it would be a confidence trick if I did."

I, on the other hand, was—still am—a fine figure of a woman, to use the old-fashioned term. Five foot nine, good firm figure, incredibly well-shaped legs. I'd look good in any East End pub, and I'd have blokes coming up to me if I was on my own. In fact, that had been the story of my life since I was a well-developed sixteen.

"I hate the way his family's looking down on you," said my friend Val to me in the ladies', as the wedding wound down to its final whimper. "It's Sam who's getting the best deal, marrying you."

"Course it is," I said calmly, piling on the lipstick. "It's no fun having a little runt like that scrambling round on top of you."

I should have checked the cubicles. His sister emerged and marched out, her face rhododendron pink.

"Ooops!" I said. "Naughty me!"

You will have guessed by now that I was not making a marriage of love. Probably you will have assumed that I married Sam for his money, but that wasn't in fact the heart of the matter. Oh, I could spend money with the best of them, and enjoy myself while I was doing it, but what I really loved, and love, was the process of making money. I liked managing a business, watching it grow, adding more businesses, amalgamating, leading at the end of it all to a business *empire*. I knew I had a wonderful commercial brain. Whatever happened, I would prosper in the world. By marrying Sam I merely cut out the first rungs of the ladder, starting out at a point where I could give adequate opportunities to my gifts.

I had worked in one of Sam's little chain stores, all called Occasionals, when I was a teenager. I'd left for a spell in a big London department store, where I had learnt to hide my commonness under a genteel mask when the occasion demanded—though never getting rid of the hardness that went with the commonness, for that would have been fatal to my ambitions. When I was twenty-four, and ready for my first moves up the ladder, I met Sam again in an East London pub, the Old Mare.

"Well, hello, Mr. Kopinski. Long time no see!"

His eyes lit up at the sight of me. Sam was always excited by large, well-formed women, particularly young ones. But having smiled, he frowned.

"Lovely to see you again too, Miss . . . er, I don't quite remember your—"

"Your Walthamstow branch. I was just a slip of a thing. Remember now?"

"Ah yes! Miss—"

"Hayton. Maggie-Lou Hayton."

"Of course," he lied. "I remember you well. Always knew you'd go far."

So that was how it had begun. I should add that I'd gone to work at Occasionals because I saw the chain's potential, and I'd never changed my opinion while working in central London. Furthermore I knew the Old Mare was Sam Kopinski's favorite pub, and that he was always there early on a Wednesday evening, which was why I was there to meet up with him. You have to make your chances in life, that's what I believe. Waiting for them to come to you is for wimps. The first move was mine, and mine was all the running thereafter.

I was twenty-six when we married. We'd been living together for eighteen months, and I knew Sam through and through. I wouldn't have married him if I hadn't already made some suggestions on business matters, seen him consider them seriously, then act on them. When we got back from the honeymoon (which was in Brighton, because Sam hated "abroad," and loved going to swish hotels with his king-size prize on his arm—or more accurately with him on mine), I lost no time in involving myself in the business. I went around with him to the different branches of Occasionals, sussed out the tastes of the various locations they were situated in, and made suggestions about stock, staffing, moves toward a different market. Sam already knew I had a flair. Soon he began to say I had a sort of genius.

"I just don't know what I'd do without you now," he often said.

In point of fact his doing without me was not at all what I envisioned for the future.

I quite soon became a sort of fixture—a power that the shop managers had to reckon with. If Sam couldn't pay his regular visit—because of a board meeting, a business deal or whatever—I went instead. Most of the managers would very much rather have had Sam than me, but one or two of them recognized a kindred soul in me, understood what I was trying to do with the business, and I noted them down for preferment when the time came.

It was the moment for the firm to be branching out, diversifying, developing other interests. Sam saw that, but he was too timid to act on it. It was me who gave him the backbone. "What else do I know about but clothes?" he would wail. "What else do *we* know about?" I corrected him. We bought into a small chain of jewelers specializing in Oriental pieces, a firm of delicatessens based in Hampstead and one or two other things. We were testing the waters, enlarging my experience.

And so things went on for a year, eighteen months. I had a timetable, and I didn't envisage rushing things. It's people who rush things who get caught out, one way or another. Apart from the expansion of the business I wanted gradually to detach Sam from his hoity-toity family. I didn't want any of the loot willed in their direction on the principle of "to them that hath." Though oddly enough it was after only a few months of marriage that one night, when we were smooching away in front of late-night television, Sam said:

"You've made me so happy, do you know that? There isn't anybody else in the world could have made me so happy. I'm going to make a new will tomorrow leaving everything to you. So there's no questions, or nastiness."

And he was as good as his word. In a couple of days' time he showed me a copy, entrusted it to me. I did question in my mind whether that was a will designed to prevent any nastiness after his death, but I gave him a big sloppy kiss and kept quiet about that. I could cope with the Kopinskis in all their ramifications.

But, as I say, I was in no hurry. I would have been happy to stay married to Sam three, four, even five years, so as to get every detail of the business under my belt, under my skin. Even in the eighteen months I had got various friends and like minds into positions of responsibility, including a job for

Val in the small PR department at the head office. So when fate struck, at a party there, Val was present to witness it.

It was a party to celebrate a tie-up between Occasionals and a production company, Banglawear—a British company which used the cheap labor of Bangladeshi women living in Britain. It was a neat, lean operation, and the tie-up had great possibilities. I was the hostess at the party, but everybody there knew I was also one of the brains behind the expansion of Kopinski Limited. Sam and I were standing by the food table watching the throng when a man came up.

"Wonderful party—just what was needed to get this off the ground," he said. "You're lucky, Sam—your wife's not only beautiful, but she's got a fine business brain as well."

And that was it. It may have been his voice—cockney, but softened, rather like mine. It may have been the fact that he was six foot three, with strong shoulders, dark wavy hair and a square chin. I always did like my men, when there was a choice, big. Whatever it was, I knew that this was him, this was the man I had to have.

"Here," said Sam, chuckling, "I'm not sure I like my business associates making up to my wife in public."

I folded him to my midriff, mussing his hair, and looked at the man. Val was watching us. She says that when she saw that look she knew that Sam was a goner.

His name, I found out very quickly, was Wayne Donovan. He was officially the head accountant, actually the creative financial brain behind Banglawear. I made sure I rang him the next day on business. By the end of the week we were lovers.

Sam never knew, I'm quite sure of that. I told him shortly after Wayne bedded me for the first time that what I needed to do was an economics diploma.

"What do you want with one of them?" he demanded. "I've never felt the need."

"I've got to see the larger picture," I said. "I understand about cash flow, diversification, things like that, but I need to get the context."

Nothing could have been further from the truth. My business sense is pure instinct, and I don't need any poncy professors pushing their theories at me. Still, it served its turn. I was out three evenings a week, and though I was learning a lot I wasn't sitting in any lecture room. That left four evenings, and I was always especially loving to Sam on those four. I don't know how I found the strength.

Wayne was a wonderful lover. He was full of surprises— and I don't just mean what you think I mean either. Even out of bed he always seemed to have something up his sleeve, something that would make every evening I spent with him special. One time he hired the most wonderful little Oriental pair to prepare a Chinese banquet for two. Another time, on a fine midsummer evening, he drove us down to Kent and we had a balloon trip over the Channel. Once, when we were eating on the balcony of a first-rate eatery in Yorkshire somewhere, he had the local colliery brass band along to serenade us. That was since we were married, when we haven't had to be discreet. It's been a great liberation for Wayne: it's as if he wants to tell the whole wide world how much he loves me. Could a girl ask for more?

Wayne says he grew up on the toughest council estate in East London, and I can believe him. You don't come from that sort of background and get to where he's got without making some pretty dodgy acquaintances along the way. When, after three months of ecstatic loving, and when I was quite sure of my man, I broached the subject of Sam, Wayne just said: "You leave that to me. I've got mates who'll take care of him. But it'll cost you a couple of thou."

The cheapness of it took my breath away.

"I can spend that on a party dress," I said. "Are you sure you're getting the best?"

"The best money can buy. Start thinking about your widow's weeds."

It was beginning to be urgent. I'd realized a day or two before that I was pregnant. Sam would never have imagined it could be anyone's but his, but I didn't want his bloody family starting to pry into my affairs, which they might if I produced a six-foot-three baby. I wanted Sam well out of the way before it was born. Wayne and I discussed a hit-and-run, but in the end we decided on an armed robbery that went wrong. For a potbellied runt Sam was remarkably careless about carrying large sums of money. Regularly once a month we would go to the Casino down the road from the head office and he'd carry with him a hefty wad of cash. It was quite unnecessary but I think it excited him. Normally I'd be with him: casinos are my kind of place. That month I pleaded off.

"I've got this nagging headache," I said. "Do you know, I think I could be pregnant."

So Sam died happy as a sandboy. When the police came to tell me I wailed: "If only I'd gone with him. They'd never have attacked him if I'd been with him." Too bloody right they wouldn't!

There I was, then, a merry widow, and the only problem was not letting the merriness show. I behaved admirably at the funeral, and if Sam's family let themselves down by showing their greed and suspicion—well, it reflected only on them, not on me. It was a good ten days after his death before I went in to work and resumed the reins, this time riding solo.

Not that I intended riding solo for long.

Quite soon after taking over I decided that the tie-up with Banglawear was so successful that it should be strengthened and extended. That meant a great deal of consultation with their chief accountant. People got used to his being in and out of the office, to our lunching together, even going off together in the evening. I expect Val made a few meaningful remarks, so everyone was prepared for the inevitable.

We got married very quietly. In fact, it was downright secretive, if you want to know the truth. I intended Sam's family to be presented with a fait accompli. I wrote the day after to Sam's sister saying I couldn't bear the thought of the baby growing up without a father. In the office I varied this slightly. "I want the baby to have a father," I said. "And quite apart from that, he's so gorgeous. . . ." Because no one who had seen Wayne would think I married him just as a father for my unborn child.

"Oh, the baby will have a father all right," Val said to me in private. "I wouldn't bother with the 'step' bit if I were you."

I like Val. She's sharp like me. I slip her a thousand now and then on top of her wages. Of course, she *knows* nothing, but I like to have her on my side.

Wayne was delighted when the baby came. Not that he's one of those modern fathers who practically claim a fifty percent stake in the pregnancy, hold your hand during labor and spend all their time bathing the baby and changing nappies afterward. He's old-fashioned. He thinks that's woman's work, so we got an au pair, a sparkling little Italian girl called Renata. It means there's never any problem with our working all day, and we can even get off on weekends alone together. Don't get the idea I don't love little Stephen, though, just because I'm not going to let him interfere with my career. I dote on him. If I'm working late at the office I often phone Renata and tell her to bring him in, so I can have a bit of time with him. She brought him in yesterday at the end of a party we threw for the top people of a PR firm we're starting to use. When I saw him I just threw my arms around him and kissed his little face. It must have made very good PR.

"This is the man in my life!" I said to the guests.

"Here—where does that leave me?" Wayne asked humorously.

I bundled Stephen back to Renata and buried my face in his marvelous chest.

"All right—he's the baby in my life. There's only one man in my life, and that's you till the day I die!"

I sensed that Wayne was looking at Renata, probably to put her and the baby in their proper places. He *is* the only man in my life, and I'm the only woman in his.

We're going away this weekend—some secret destination Wayne has worked out. I expect he's got some tremendous surprise lined up for me as part of it. Val has left a message on my answering machine saying to ring her urgently, but it'll do when we get back. If she wants more money she's not going to get it. You can overstep the bounds of friendship. And all she's got to go on is just a *look*—and you can't make evidence out of a look. It doesn't bother me at all. I'm going to concentrate on wonderful Wayne and the surprise he'll have waiting for me this weekend.

HAPPY CHRISTMAS

"*T*he people I'm sorry for at Christmas are the ones with children," said Crespin Fawkes, in a voice that penetrated to the farthest corners of The Wagon of Hay. "It must be dreadful for them."

He looked around his group of listeners from the corners of his bright little eyes, registering their appreciative chuckles. Then he took another sip of his vodka and tonic.

"Think of it: the noise, the toy trumpets, the crackers and the computer games! Much more appropriate, one would have thought, as a celebration of the crucifixion!"

This time the appreciation was more muted. The joke would have been better if he had left it alone. Crespin never had been able to leave a good thing alone.

But they had all enjoyed the joke, and like all good jokes it went home to them. They all, in their way, faced a future when their Christmases would be alone. The Wagon of Hay was one of those pubs where what are today called the sexual minorities tended to congregate. Several of Crespin's group were old boyfriends of his, or occasional partners, and most of the ones who weren't were so because Crespin had very definite ideas about what he fancied and what he didn't. Then there were Joan and Evelyn, who definitely had a relationship, but who enjoyed male company; and there was Patty, whom nobody could quite pin down.

Still, the fact was that they were all, except Crespin, young or youngish. Almost all of them would in fact be going home to families for Christmas, however much they might profess boredom, reluctance or irritation. Joan, or Evelyn, would ring home and say: "Can I bring my flatmate?" and Mummy would say: "Of *course,* dear!" The others would go on their own, probably, bearing sophisticated presents from the metropolis. For three or four days they would be back in the bosoms of their families, cherished and chaste. When you got to Crespin's age you didn't have a family with a bosom to go back to, but that was something in the future for the rest of them. Crespin had always preferred to keep company with young people.

"You're not going down to your sister, then?" asked Gregory.

"My dears, *no!*" said Crespin, with a theatrical shudder. "Not after last time. And to be perfectly frank, she didn't ask me. She has teenage boys, and the fact is she doesn't trust me with them, though last time I saw them they promised to be both pudgy and spotty, which is something I can't *abide.* But a mother can't see that her children are positively off-putting. And Priscilla's house and grounds are positively country gentry, which is not *me* at all: you expect to see Mummers on Christmas Eve, all madly tugging at their forelocks and talking Thomas Hardy. 'Thank 'ee koindly, squoire'—all that stuff. Oh dear, no. Not even for a twenty-pound turkey with all the trimmings would I betake myself to Priscilla's. I *much* prefer my own company, and *la cuisine de chez Marks et Sparks!*"

Once more there was a gratifying laugh. Crespin sat back in his seat, his performance over for a few minutes, as he let the younger ones take over. As their talk about who was going with whom washed over him (Crespin had had a lifetime of who was going with whom, had figured in it as often as not), he let his eye rove around the bar. There were the Chelsea locals—for there was a straight clientele as well—there were the blacks, the lesbians, the kinks and the rough trade—these last all friends of Crespin's.

And there, over by the bar, was a boy by himself. Boy? Young man? Somewhere on the border, Crespin judged him. He was eyeing the company speculatively—listening, absorbing. His shirt, dazzling white, looked as if it had been bought that day, but his cardigan, which he had taken off and draped over his arm, was pure home-knit, his jeans were chain-store, and his shoes might have been bought for him by his mother for his last year at school. There was about him an indefinable air of newly-up-from-the-country. As Crespin looked at that face, intently absorbing the ambience of The Wagon of Hay, it suddenly struck him that he'd seen it before, knew it, if only slightly—that somewhere or other he had come across this young man as a child.

The young man's eyes, roving around the bar, suddenly met his, and there seemed to Crespin to come into them a flash of recognition. Then he turned to the landlord and ordered a fresh half of lager. Crespin turned back to his friends. This was the last Saturday before Christmas. He wouldn't see them again for quite a while, and the stimulus of their laughter and admiration would be missed. Crespin did need, more so as he got older, laughter and admiration. As for the young man—well, no doubt an opportunity would present itself. It so often did, Crespin found.

In the event, it wasn't so much opportunity that presented itself as the young man himself—"on a plate, as it were," as Crespin said wonderingly to him. There was a ring on his doorbell on Christmas Eve, and there on the doormat he stood—dark-haired, thick-eyebrowed, strong-shouldered—altogether . . . capable. Crespin warmed to him at once, to the mere sight of him, and smiled his very friendliest smile.

"I hope you'll excuse me bothering you," said the young man. "I saw you in the Wagon the other night, you see—"

"And *I* saw *you*," said Crespin.

"And I saw you in the street the other day too—you didn't see me—and I followed you here."

"Flattering," said Crespin. "Almost invariably, nowadays, it's the other way round."

"You see, I think I know you. Met you once or twice, years ago. And your picture's on your sister's piano. The boys are always saying: 'That's our uncle, who's in television.' "

"So much more distinguished than 'who's *on* television,' though whether *they* appreciate that is another matter. Are you sure that's *all* they say?"

The boy smiled, twisting his mouth.

" 'That's our uncle, who's queer and in television.' "

"Exactly. Don't bother with the censored version. But this leads to the delicious question of who *you* are."

"My father's the gardener. I always used to help him, in the school holidays. That's how I met you."

By now they were both in the hallway of Crespin's awfully amusing flat, and quite naturally Crespin had removed the boy's duffel coat and taken his inadequate scarf. They understood each other so well that no invitation, no pantomime of reluctance, hardly, even, any meaningful looks had been necessary. Quite soon the boy was sitting on the sofa, with Crespin in the armchair close beside him, and they were both clutching drinks and talking about anything but what Crespin really wanted to talk about, and the boy's eyes were going everywhere. For all that there were slight traces of the bumpkin about him, Crespin decided at once that he was an awfully noticing boy. There was almost nothing in Crespin's living room that escaped his wandering eye.

"You like it? My little nest, I mean."

"Yes, awfully. It's not like what I'm used to. Even at your sister's—"

"My *dear*, I should think not! Don't even *men*tion my sister's in the same breath if you want to stay in favor! Of course, she has the odd good *piece*—could hardly fail to have in a house as old as that—but everything that she's bought herself has been the purest Home Counties. Now *I* rediscovered the thirties ten or fifteen years before anyone else. I bought, bought, bought, quite ri*di*culously cheaply, dear boy. I wouldn't like to tell you what some of the things are worth today."

As he said it, Crespin noticed on those sturdy country features a registering twitch, a gleam in the eye.

"This Beaton, for example. *Only* a photograph, my dear, but in its original frame, and signed to the subject, who was a *quite* minor poet—well, someone offered me four hundred and fifty only the other day. And I paid two bob for it, back in the days of Harold Macmillan, in a little shop in East Finchley."

All the time the boy's eyes were watching, waiting for him to go on to another item. Crespin, characteristically, decided to play with him. He sat down beside him on the sofa.

"But don't let's talk about my little knickknacks. Let's talk about you. I don't even know your name."

His name, it turned out, was Stephen Hodge.

At home, he said, things hadn't been "all that bad," but on the other hand he hadn't got on "all that well" with his parents. His father had been old-fashioned and heavy-handed, and had insisted on his leaving school at sixteen. "Don't want you loafing around there for the rest of your life, learning things that won't be no use to you," he had said. Stephen had wanted to stay on. He was middling at most things, but he had a definite talent in certain directions: "Art and that," he said. He had wanted to get an education to get away from home, find new horizons, "meet exciting people," he said. And he added: "Get new experiences."

By now they were in the kitchen, and Crespin was preparing one of his risottos.

"Something light," he said. "We want to keep our appetites for tomorrow."

Over the risotto, Crespin returned to the absorbing topic—absorbing, in fact, to both of them—of his flat, his possessions.

"When we've eaten, dear boy, you shall have a tour of the flat. A personal conducted tour, led by the chatelaine. Then you can feel truly at home here for the festive season. Where are you living, as a rule?"

"I've got this camp bed at a mate's," said Stephen, eating hungrily as if he had little desire to save his appetite for the morrow. "He's away for Christmas."

"Then we are saving each other from some perfectly ghastly festive days. I shall conduct you round my nest and my *things*, so that you will know them as you will know me." He smiled at the boy, who slowed down the pace of his eating. "I can see that you have an eye for fine things."

This last was said with a touch of malice, but it went unperceived. The boy said:

"I think I do. But I don't have the training and that. I need someone to show me."

After Crespin had found some ice cream in the fridge, which Stephen wolfed up in a way that suggested the schoolboy that showed through some of his clothes, Crespin put on some coffee and they began the conducted tour of the flat. The eye that Crespin had noticed almost from the beginning went everywhere, and the brain stored every item of information. The living room was thirties, but the rest of the flat was pleasantly crowded with more conventional objects of all kinds and dates. Often Crespin noticed that Stephen wanted to ask the value of something, but managed to refrain. Sometimes Crespin would give it to him, sometimes not. He began to drop prices and sale values into his patter, but ambiguously ("Would you believe me if I said fifteen hundred?"). He was already playing with his guest—beginning the games that would be conducted more roughly in the bedroom.

Soon a refinement of the game suggested itself to him. Instead of being ambiguous, his assertions of value became downright mendacious. His valuable things—oh yes, ducky, he did *have* valuable things—were commended as amusing trifles, no more. The highest commendation and implied value were lavished on pieces whose worth was at best sentimental.

If *that*, said Crespin to himself, as he held—gently, as if it were Ming, and he a museum curator—a piece of nondescript china inherited from his Aunt Molly, which looked as if it had been purchased from Woolworth's in the twenties.

"*Ex*quisite," said Crespin. "And beautifully kept, you notice. Trust my Aunt Molly for that, dragon that she was. I wouldn't like to tell you what my friend Henry at Chez Moi Antiques round the corner would offer me for that, if I ever told him I'd sell."

He saw the boy, in some space behind his eyes, file the information away. For a moment Crespin felt himself washed by a wave of nausea and ennui. So many young men—tough, capable, greedy. So many nights of delicious brutality, followed by less delicious humiliation, depredation, loss. He shrugged the feeling aside, and went on with the tour. Crespin was a magpie. Only a fraction of his things could be shown that evening. There would be plenty left to talk about the next day.

After coffee, and after all the china and glass had been safely tucked away inside the dishwasher, the games started again, but this time they were more physical, and this time it was Crespin who was the victim. And in these games Stephen understood what was going on. It was amazing how quickly he got the idea. But then, he had been in London some weeks. Crespin had no reason to think he was the first of his kind that the boy had been with. If he frequented The Wagon of Hay, after all . . .

But it was a pleasure to encounter a lad with that sturdiness of physique, yet with that delicate inventiveness of mind. They started with the schoolboy stuff, with the arm twisted behind the back, but then they proceeded, sometimes Crespin suggesting, sometimes Stephen improvising, to more serious brutalities. Halfway through the games, both of them sweaty, Crespin a little bloody, they stopped for a neat scotch. By this time they had very little in the way of clothes on, and some of Crespin's, lying on the floor, were torn and dirty. As he drained his glass Crespin plunged his other hand down Stephen's schoolboyish Y-fronts, and the games began again, until they climaxed, gloriously, on the bed, Stephen's big hands around Crespin's throat as he lay on top of him.

"It's been one of the most wonderful nights of my life," Crespin said, after Stephen had roughly taken him for the second time.

The next morning Crespin was up early, showering away the dried blood, and gazing with satisfaction at the discoloration of his skin as bruises began to show. Before going into the kitchen he went through the lounge and drawing room, looking for something sufficiently masculine to present to Stephen on Our Lord's birthday. He found nothing that satisfied him, and in the end wrapped up a really beautiful Georgian silver cream jug. In his gifts, at least, he would be generous, he thought. He made tea and toast, set out the tray for two, then put the present on the tray and went into the bedroom. Stephen was awake and sitting up. Crespin thought he had never seen anything more beautiful. He set the tray on the boy's lap, presented him with the little parcel, then sat himself cross-legged on the end of the bed.

"It's beautiful, really beautiful," Stephen said, gazing at the silver object.

"Nothing—a mere nothing," said Crespin, with his characteristic wave of the hand.

"And I have nothing to give you."

"Do you imagine you could give me anything more wonderful than you have given me already?" asked Crespin. Stephen looked pleased, and Crespin added: "Dear boy . . ."

They had a quiet morning preparing the lunch. The cookery of Mrs. Marks and Mrs. Sparks did not need long in the oven—Crespin was pleased to find that he had *two* packets of stuffed turkey breast in the deep freeze. He would feed Stephen up. He knew the boy was hungrier than, so far, he had been able to satisfy. He peeled a mountain of potatoes and carrots, set out the cranberry sauce on a pretty Meissen dish, opened the tin of National Trust Christmas pudding. Stephen's eyes sparkled at this: he still had a child's love of sweet things. While this was going on, Stephen did his bit around the place, clearing up from the night before and setting the table, at which he proved surprisingly adept. In between they watched bits of the Christmas morning service on television.

"Are you religious?" asked Stephen.

"I converted to Rome when I was eighteen," said Crespin, with some signs of pride. "Inevitably, with my name, I suppose. Such a relief after the middle-of-the-road Anglicanism of my childhood—the middle of the road down which my dear sister and her family still happily plod. But somehow the conversion didn't last. Too much an impulse of emotion, I'm afraid, of theatricality. I regret it. And you?"

"I don't know. I don't go to church and that. But sometimes I watch it on television and it seems to . . . have something. But I'm not religious. It doesn't sort of . . . go, does it?"

"Go?"

"With us. With the sort of lives we lead."

"No," agreed Crespin sadly. Soon he went back to the kitchen.

They ate about two o'clock. The meal was a great success. Stephen ate about two thirds of the turkey, and was clearly pleased with a Christmas dinner that was all breast and no leg or wing. He made significant inroads into the vegetables, and seemed to enjoy Crespin's cream on the Christmas pudding in place of the custard he always had at home. Before the meal they had a glass of sherry—Reina Victoria. Stephen said it was like no sherry he had ever had before, inspected the bottle and asked how much it cost. As they ate, Crespin gave him a little lecture on Moselles. How often had he given it before, over dinner, to a bored, contemptuous or frankly dim-witted companion? Stephen followed him, asked questions, stored up the answers.

He will take everything I have to give him, thought Crespin.

"Do you want to ring your family?" he asked.

"No," said Stephen awkwardly. "No. They don't know where I am, you see."

"I'm not pressing you. That's your business."

"Will you be ringing your sister? Don't say anything if so."

"I shan't ring her. She won't be expecting it. Nobody will. Outside my job I have nobody." Crespin paused, then said deliberately: "I could lie here, dead, for days, weeks, and nobody would know. . . ."

He registered, unmistakably, a tiny glint in the boy's eye.

They went back to the living room for coffee, and as he poured it and handed his to Stephen, Crespin said: "This has been a Christmas to remember."

"For me too," said Stephen.

"Two days, wonderfully marked off from the humdrum round."

"Maybe we could do it again."

"Dear boy, *repetition*, even if it were possible, is not advisable. Exquisite pleasure is a once-off thing. With your inventive mind you should understand that."

Stephen smiled slowly.

"You think I have an inventive mind?"

"I know you have. I'm in a position to pronounce on the subject."

Stephen stirred his coffee.

"I could stay."

"Dear boy!" cried Crespin, fluttering his hand. "Do you imagine I could stand excitements like last night's every day?"

"We wouldn't need to go at it like that every day."

"If you were here, *with* me, how could we not? Come, you've never seen my study. Let me continue with your aesthetic education."

So Crespin resumed yesterday's game, with renewed zest. He had the boy at an ideal stage: he was quick but ignorant. In a year's time—if he remained at large—this particular fun would no longer be possible. He would *know*. Now he was anxious to learn, but did not know. Thus Crespin could wave aside a rare, intimate conversation piece by John Singer Sargent which hung over the mantelpiece as "a mere daub, dear boy. Hardly worth the canvas and oil. Though I keep it for sentimental reasons."

He paused, as an idea seemed to strike him. He looked up at the stalwart man, the worried wife and the three girls of the picture.

"My great-grandfather, the Admiral. And his three jollytar daughters. Imagine—that his blood should have diluted itself into mine. Funnily enough, I remember one of the daughters, in old age, chivvying me into manly sports. The Admiral, I always suspect, would have gone in for more drastic remedies. Probably have had me drowned at birth. He was never one for half measures."

Crespin, watched by the boy, tore his eyes from the exquisite "daub" over the fireplace and took, very casually, from the top of a bureau a large, silver-encrusted nineteenth-century firearm.

"This was his. Isn't it handsome? And characteristically assertive. Feel the weight of it."

The boy took it, and in his surprise nearly dropped it. It was as heavy as Death.

"It's not a gun at all, in fact. Really more of a cudgel. He had it made to his own specifications. He always said that if you shot an intruder some damn fool was going to ask questions. With this you could either terrify him or bash the daylights out of him if it didn't work." Crespin looked at Stephen, and took the weapon from his hands. "It's one of the best pieces I own. I always think it might come in useful someday, to somebody."

Their glance at each other held a brief flash of understanding. Then they went on to other things. As before, Crespin praised dreary cut-glass vases and commercial prints as if they were priceless objects the Victoria and Albert were itching to get their hands on. The pleasure was redoubled because, in addition to observing that pricing-and-cataloguing routine going on behind the boy's eyes, he had a sense of something more too: of the boy screwing himself up to something. When he put his hand on his arm, or delicately round his waist, he could feel it as already manifesting itself physically in a bodily tenseness.

Those brief touches, those affectionate squeezes, inevitably began to lead to something more, but Crespin was not anxious to start on the serious business yet. He wanted a cup of tea. He had always enjoyed tea, and served it in a ceremonious way that reminded him of his mother. He would enjoy one more cup.

The boy's tensions had relaxed by the time they both drank tea. For a moment Crespin wondered whether he had changed his mind, but he was reassured to notice a tiny smile of anticipation playing around his lips: he was relaxed because he had decided to do it.

Conversation between them was strained and spasmodic, as it had never been since Stephen had arrived. Now they had between them an unspoken contract. Any mention of it could only render it ludicrous and void. So they must talk about other things, though other things scarcely came. In the end Crespin put an end to it after one cup. Second cups were always less than perfect. He turned toward the boy beside him on the sofa, and began gently to unbutton his shirt. Stephen, at least, must look kempt when he left the flat.

His own clothes were another matter. God knew, he had not exactly been cautious in the past. Now there was nothing he wore that could mean anything to him again. But as the game hotted up, no item was given up without a struggle. The shirt went as he was held back forcefully over the sofa, his head being pummeled by one fist as the boy's other hand tore at the flaunting pink silk. Other items went as they fought across the table, chased each other round the kitchen, sank into violent clinches onto the floor. There were intervals of something like tenderness, almost peace, as their naked bodies came together in something other than struggle. There was a moment, on the rug, in front of the gas fire, when it almost seemed as if the contract between them might be forgotten. It was Crespin who ended it. He slapped Stephen ineffectually across the cheeks.

"Pig!" he shouted. "Yokel! Rustic yob!"

Stephen's fists began brutally hitting him about the head, first left, then right, leaving Crespin breathless. Then Stephen unclenched his hands and felt for the throat. It was a feeling that had always excited Crespin, but he knew that this time he could not give way to his excitement. That was not the way he had to go. It had to be by the Admiral's gun. He writhed on the rug, twisted and turned within those strong hands. The bodies came together, then slid off one another, until suddenly Crespin managed to knee the boy in the groin. With a wrench he struggled away as Stephen let go his hands, then he ran for the bedroom.

"Come for me!" he shouted. "Come for me!"

He slammed the door, but it swung open again. He stood there in the darkness, panting, aching, watching the light from the living room as it filtered through the opening in the doorway. The boy was not coming. Wait. He heard a floor-board creak. The one just inside the study door. He was going for the weapon. Perhaps he was looking round—at the things he would take, the things he had marked off in his little inventory, the things that would fetch the odd pound merely when he hawked them round the antique shops, as soon as he dared.

Crespin's breath was coming more easily now. Let him come! Let him not break the rhythm! He heard the floor-board creak again. He heard soft footsteps across the carpeted floor of the living room. He was coming after all. The game would be played through.

And as he saw, in the lighted doorway of the bedroom, a large, dark shadow, there flooded over him an overwhelming feeling of excitement and fulfillment. It had been the happiest Christmas of his adult life.

READER, I STRANGLED HIM

The restoration of Mr. Rochester's sight, as I remarked to the rector of Ferndean village, was indeed a blessing. The rector is a man of conventional mind and limited imagination, so I did not add that, like most blessings, it was not unmixed.

Mr. Rochester's past life had been narrated to me in all its thrilling, shocking detail by the firelight at Thornfield some years before. I cannot therefore pretend that his nature was a closed book to me. While my husband's optic orbs were bleared and clouded I was his sight: I led him, I described objects and weathers to him, I expounded from the public prints the thrilling events of the day—Napoleon's return from Elba, his hundred days of restored power, his defeat by our country's incomparable hero at Waterloo. By the time the Bourbon monarch was once more uncertainly in the saddle in Paris my husband's eyes were beginning to discern light, shapes, even colors. When our son began to walk his father could lead him around the garden unaided by me. By the time the Prince Regent became sovereign de jure as well as de facto Edward Fairfax Rochester could read, write, and do everything of importance for himself. My importance in his life was greatly diminished.

And as his eyes cleared, so they began to roam: to wander, notice, and choose.

Let me be clear: I have never admired bloodless men. I counted myself fortunate to have married a man well versed

in matters of the heart and in their physical expression. To be
with him was both thrilling in itself and educational. I could
even, I think, have tolerated occasional episodes with house-
maids and suchlike, as the expression of a nature hot and
unaccustomed to the restraints of convention.

But there are limits. An occasional episode is not to be
confused with the constant pursuit of amorous experience.
And when that constant pursuit resulted in a fading interest
in his own wife, then my lamentations were bitter indeed.
Now my visits to Ferndean village were marked by encounters with rustic maidens—*girls*—who curtsied to me with
their eyes fixed firmly on the ground. Nay, there were some
who, when they thought they were past me, smirked. My
position in the county, never secure by reason of my past as an
educator of young ladies, became shaky indeed.

I made my unhappiness clear to Edward.

"I shall take Fairfax and go and live on one of your other properties," I said. "That way I shall avoid constant humiliation."

"You will do nothing of the sort," he said in his abrupt way.
"That boy is the light of my life."

"I was once your light, and your eyes," I said bitterly.

"You are still, my sprite," he said, caressing my hand. "But
now there are lesser lights."

I snatched my hand away.

"Then I will go and live somewhere with Fairfax on my
own inheritance."

"You have no inheritance. You and I made no settlement
before marriage. And a woman has no rights to her children."

I subsided into impotent rage, for he spoke no more than
the legal, immoral truth.

I was similarly worsted when, some time later, he brought
up the subject of young Fairfax's education.

"Time we thought of a governess for the lad," he said one day at dinner.

"A governess! But I am quite capable of teaching Fairfax."

"You think so, my dear? My son needs more than charity-school learning. Besides, you are my wife, with your own duties. It would hardly help your position in the county to remind people of what you once were."

"My position in the county has already been undermined by your exercising a *droit du seigneur* on all the girls for miles around," I said, hardly bearing to look at him.

"You talk nonsense, Jane. The *droit du seigneur* has never existed in this country."

He pronounced the phrase in the French manner to underline my inferior education, and perhaps to remind me of his extensive experience among French ladies of the most degraded type.

"By your exercising a *droit du seigneur* I mean that you use your wealth and rank to force otherwise virtuous girls to agree to your embraces," I said. He shrugged.

"You say you see them in the village. Do they look reluctant or regretful?"

Once again I was reduced to silence.

I first saw the advertisement when it appeared in the *Leeds Intelligencer* and the *Bradford Argus*. It detailed the need of a substantial family of gentlefolk in Yorkshire for an educator (female) for their "amiable and intelligent only son," and it specified a time and a place for interviews of the applicants. I had not been consulted about the advertisement, so I said to my high-handed lord: "I insist on being present at the interviews."

"Of course, my dear," he replied, meekly. "Your experience will be invaluable."

Five ladies came for the interview. Naturally my preference was for the quietest, most downtrodden of them. My choice, however, for various reasons, was for Mrs. Nelson, an elderly lady of forbidding mien but firm of manner and with strong religious principles. The one I feared most was Miss Grey, whose quiet, demure manner masked the fact that she had a pretty face and an inviting eye.

"Mrs. Nelson," I said when they had gone, "is undoubtedly the best candidate. She has far more experience than the rest, and will correct any tendency to willfulness in the boy."

"My sentiments entirely," Edward said, to my surprise. "The good Mrs. Nelson it shall be. With Miss Grey in reserve."

I wrote the letter for him to Mrs. Nelson. How he organized it I do not know, but within the week we had had a reply regretfully declining the position, as she had had an offer which she could not refuse from the Yorkshire nobility.

Edward wrote the letter to Miss Grey himself.

Miss Grey replied accepting the post, but pleading that she be allowed to delay taking it up until her present charge should be ready to go to public school in September. Edward replied that the delay was no great matter, and we looked forward to welcoming her to Ferndean Manor as soon as was convenient to her.

The delay at least gave me time to plan. However, no plan could I come up with.

It must be said that as the weeks wore on and I was still unable to think of a strategy to prevent Miss Grey coming to Ferndean, or to prevent the near-inevitable when she did, my nerves became more than a little frayed. I was shrewish to my husband, which he richly deserved, but I was an irritable, distrait mother to young Fairfax, which he didn't. Thus matters stood one warm evening in early August when the jangling of a bell announced a visitor. I was in the library, teaching Fairfax his first steps in arithmetic, when I heard John approach my husband in the sitting room.

"Good Lord!" I heard him say. Then he got up and went to the door that led to the hallway. "Mason! My good man! It's a tonic to see you!"

My heart sank. Those last words must surely have been ironic. It was never a tonic to see Mr. Mason, least of all for me. This pathetic, irresolute, unmanly creature was the person who had stepped in to prevent my marriage to Mr. Rochester when first he attempted to make me his, in Hay Church. I should no doubt have been grateful to him, for preventing my becoming a bigamous bride, but truth to tell I felt only aversion for the man.

"But what brings you here?" I heard my husband ask, after the bustle of welcome.

"I was in the county, wandering about at will, and the nearness of Ferndean made me irresistibly anxious to see"—he paused; I waited—"my old friend and brother-in-law Edward Fairfax Rochester."

I had no doubt what in fact he had come to see. It was time that he saw it—saw me. I went to the sitting room with young Fairfax.

"Mr. Mason. I am pleased to make your acquaintance again. This is Mr. Rochester's son and heir. Time for bed now, Fairfax. I shall be up in a minute or two. Now, you will stay to supper, Mr. Mason?"

"He will stay the night, and as many nights as he can," said my lord.

He engaged to stay that night only, and I hoped that was all I should be subjected to. He was the same unhealthy, unsatisfactory man he had been when I first saw him. His desire to see me as lady of the house, rather than the family's obscure governess, did not advance him in my good opinion. Over dinner he attempted compliments, beginning with young Fairfax.

"A fine boy, that I could see. A manly boy."

"I am endeavoring to make him into a man of *principle*," I said quietly.

"And you, Mrs. Rochester—you clearly do a wonderful job in filling poor Bertha's place."

"There was no place that your sister filled," I said tartly.

"Oh, but she was a lovely creature, when I saw her first," said Mr. Rochester, stretching in his chair. Once I would have known that he was regarding me out of the corner of his eye, having only said such a thing to produce a reaction in me. Now I no longer knew whether he was sincere or not. Thus does marriage increase our uncertainty about our spouses.

They turned then to talk of the fall in the price of coffee and sugar, and when I said that the price of these commodities from the provision merchants was still as high as ever they looked at me pityingly and Edward explained that there was no immediate connection between the two prices. Then he turned back to Mr. Mason and continued to discuss male topics into which female interventions would be unwelcome. It was clear that he found Mason a more valued guest than he ever had in the past. Formerly he had felt mostly aggravation with the man, or at best a bored tolerance of him. Perhaps it was the lack of male company of his own class at Ferndean that had led to the change. Indeed, apart from John (who with Mary was still our only servant, in spite of all my representations), he for the most part had no male company of any kind at all. Men of the village he took care to avoid.

It was, for me, a most disagreeable meal. When it ended I pleaded a headache, leaving them to their port, and later their brandy and cigars. I went to my room, and without assuming any night attire I lay on the bed, wept a little, slept a little, and thought.

It was toward midnight when I woke up from a doze, feeling my faculties as keen and alive as they had ever been. It was talking and laughter from downstairs that had woken me, and I realized that the window must be open. It became a craving in me to know what they were talking, what they were laughing, about. I snatched a housecoat, crept down the stairs, and slipped through a side door out into the cool, scented air of the night garden.

It was the sitting-room window that was open, though the heavy curtains were closed. I could see nothing, but I could hear. To hear was more than enough. I heard Edward's manly, treacherous voice.

"I meant what I said, and more. Bertha was a creature to arouse the passions of more lethargic souls than I. She was a fire in the loins, and I had to have her. No doubt your family wanted to ensnare me, but I was desperate to be ensnared."

"Her mental state—her potential mental state—was quite unknown to us."

"Hrrrmph! Perhaps. In any case I doubt if a doctor had sat me down and described the likely course of events it would have made a pennyworth of difference."

"And you have forgiven my intervention at Hay Church?"

"My dear fellow, knowing what you did, it was the only thing you could do. And you merely postponed the ev—the day."

"Thank you, my dear Edward. I merely did my duty, knowing what I did."

"Or thinking you knew what you did."

There was a moment's silence.

"Er . . . *thinking* I knew what I did?"

"Exactly," came my husband's slow, ironic voice. "It could not be explained at the time, of course."

"What could not be explained at the time?"

"Did it not occur to any of you in Jamaica that a hot-blooded young man, escaped from parental tyranny, might have got into other scrapes of a similar kind to the one you were preparing to entrap him into?"

"I don't understand, Edward—"

But I did! Or was beginning to!

"It could not be explained at the time of the interrupted marriage service, because it would hardly have altered the situation, but there had been a sweet little French *grisette* by the name of Amélie Labette, with whom my eighteen-year-old self went through a Catholic ceremony of undoubted legality."

"But you mean—"

"To the best of my knowledge she was still alive, still displaying to general admiration her many charms, when I married Bertha."

"And when you tried to marry your present charming partner?"

"I had no evidence she was dead. Hence my silence."

"But since then you have heard of her demise?"

The reply was a hearty—hearty—laugh.

"Mason, you are priceless! A good deed in a naughty world. Come to bed, man—I'll lead you up."

My heart pounding as though it would burst from my breast I fled down the garden. My throbbing temples pounded the message: "Unjust!" I had been trapped after all by Edward Rochester into a marriage that for all he knew was illegal. I was, as I had been so determined never to be, his concubine, his . . . I could not say the word, even to myself, but I was no better than his women in the village and the farms around.

No!—my conscience argued, angrily aroused: I was in every way better. I had been misused, deceived. It was Edward who was the misuser, the deceiver. It was Edward who was the criminal, the bigamist. He had taken my girl-hood from me, robbed me of all innocence, and he had done it lightly, cynically, jeering internally at my scruples, my prin-ciples, my religious faith.

I walked slowly back to the house. It was Edward who had destroyed my life, Edward who had played the Lovelace, Edward who had broken me on the wheel.

I looked through the window. The curtain blew in the breeze, and I saw that sitting at the table in the darkened room, in one of the high-backed chairs, was a man's figure. I slipped back in through the side door and went to the sitting room. An odor wafted to me: it was the smell of one of Edward's cigars. It was sitting on the tray on the table, still dully smoldering. I felt my anger rising. He had laughingly told his friend I was no more than a bigamous houri, and now he was contentedly chuckling over the joke with a brandy and a cigar. I fingered the girdle of my wrap, then took it off and wound one end round my wrist.

Reader, I strangled him. I crept in silence across the room, stood behind the chair in the darkness, then with sudden strength brought the cord down around his throat and pulled it tight, tight, tight, exulting in my power, despising his feeble struggles, my brain proclaiming myself revenged for the terri-ble wrong he had done me. When all struggle ceased I ran to my room, locked the door, and threw myself on my bed weeping, until at last I subsided into an exhausted sleep. What would happen now would happen.

My slumbers were drugged, yet haunted by doubts and a nameless dread. In the morning heavy footsteps, cries, unaccustomed sounds about the house forced themselves on me but did not wake me. The sun was well up when I was aroused by a peremptory banging on the door. I cringed beneath the bedclothes, reluctant more than fearful. The knocking was resumed, and then:

"Jane! Open this door, if you would not have it broken down!"

It was the voice of my husband. The doubts and dreads of the night had been confirmed—doubts born, I am sure, from the lack of resistance of the man in the sitting room. My Edward would always have resisted.

I got up and took the key from the door to my chamber, Edward of course had his own key. He unlocked the door, came in, and stood in front of it, arms folded over his massive chest, almost covering the doorway.

"So. My wife is a murderess, is she? And what had you against poor Mason? Not the old affair at Hay Church, surely?"

"I did not like Mason," I murmured. "But I meant him no harm. It was—"

"Exactly. It was me. A charming intention!"

I turned on him, with the remnants of my old fire.

"You married me, not knowing—without even bothering to try to find out—whether our marriage was a legal one or not."

"So: you listen outside windows, do you?"

"*You* can accuse me of a petty thing like that? You, a disgrace to manhood? You deserved to die. I will go to the gallows gladly."

"You deserve to, certainly. Poor Mason, disturbed by what

he had heard, goes down for a cigar—and I fear for a narcotic which is much used on his island. In his enfeebled state you strangle him, without bothering to ascertain that it is not your legal mate who is your victim as you intended. Certainly the noose would be a fit punishment."

"I shall go to my execution proclaiming my wrongs."

"All you would proclaim is your damnable inefficiency. In fact I do *not* care to have the name of Rochester dragged through the county courts and into the Newgate Calendar. It is hardly a spotless name, but it deserves better than that. Mr. Mason is already buried."

"Buried?"

"In Dixon's field. It was easy work. John and Mary are loyal as dogs, and I praise God I engaged no new servants, as you desired."

"But when inquiries are made?"

"I believe there will be none. He was in the county incognito, told no one he was coming here."

"Then what about me? May Fairfax and I go as I asked you to one of your other properties and . . . ?"

"The devil take you, woman! Haven't I told you no? Where is your sense of justice? There must be punishment, if there is to be true penitence. The attic room is ready for you."

"The attic room?"

"We have no true attics, but the old chamber at the end of the Elizabethan wing will suit admirably. I was, when a wild, stubborn boy, often locked in there. I found it roomy enough. The four walls of that chamber will be the confines of your existence from now on. I have sent for a keeper, but for now I must simply lock you away. It is imperative that my son know nothing of the crimes of his mother."

He stood aside. I saw John and Mary on the landing, with

no love in their faces, only condemnation and bewilderment. I stood up and went before them to my new prison.

※

I am very quiet here. Sometimes I read. Mr. Rochester does not shower me with books of devotion and contemplation (for hypocrisy is not one of his many faults), so I have the works of Sir Walter, novels by the author of *Pride and Prejudice* (not greatly to my liking), and other works of a lighter kind. But for much of the time I sit quietly. I think and I listen.

Sometimes I hear the voice of my dear little boy calling to his dog in the grounds. Sometimes I hear him and *her*, the hated Miss Grey, in intervals of his schooling. Once, at night, when Grace was asleep, I heard the voices and laughter of my Edward and *her*, from the sitting room. Then the blood rushed to my head and I sat there for minute after minute, enduring its pounding, wondering if I was becoming in reality mad.

Grace Poole has convinced Edward she is a reformed character. She assures him that drink never touches her lips. He believes her because he would rather not involve anyone else from the lower orders in the sad, disordered affairs of his family.

Where her drink comes from I no more than suspect. Some member of her family brings it, I believe, and conveys it to her during the Methodistical church service which she attends every Sunday. She makes good use of it at night.

Next month my dear Fairfax goes to stay with his "aunts" Diana and Mary. They have been very pressing that since I am so occupied (!) they must see him. Edward has agreed.

Next month it must be then.

I have my rush light. I have my wits about me, which Bertha never had. One night when Grace is in her usual drunken stupor I shall sally forth and . . .

I shall have no regrets for Grace, for *her*, or for myself. Least of all shall I have regrets for Edward Fairfax Rochester. I have discovered the difference between a man and a woman. Women forge ahead, progress, put the past behind them, and go onwards. Men are circular creatures, going not onwards but around, their lives becoming a dreary repetition of their old mistakes.

Put vulgarly, they never learn.

THE GENTLEMAN
IN THE LAKE

*T*here had been violent storms in the night, but the body did not come to the surface until they had died down and a watery summer sun was sending ripples of lemon and silver across the still-disturbed surface of Derwent Water. It was first seen by a little girl, clutching a plastic beaker of orange juice, who had strayed down from the small car park, over the pebbles, to the edge of the lake.

"What's that, Mummy?"

"What's what, dear?"

Her mother was wandering around, drinking in the calm, the silence, the magisterial beauty, more potent for the absence of other tourists. She was a businesswoman, and holidays in the Lakes made her question uncomfortably what she was doing with her life. She strolled down to where the water lapped on to the stones.

"*There*, Mummy. *That.*"

She looked toward the lake. A sort of bundle bobbed on the surface a hundred yards or so away. She screwed up her eyes. A sort of *tweedy* bundle. Greeny brown, like an old-fashioned gentleman's suit. As she watched she realized that she could make out, stretching out from the bundle, two lines. . . . *Legs.* She put her hand firmly on her daughter's shoulder.

"Oh, it's just an old bundle of clothes, darling. Look, there's Patch wanting to play. He has to stretch his legs too, you know."

Patch barked obligingly, and the little girl trotted off to throw his ball for him. Without hurrying the woman made her way back to the car, picked up the car phone and dialed 999.

⊗

It was late on in the previous summer that Marcia Catchpole had sat beside Sir James Harrington at a dinner party in St. John's Wood. "Something immensely distinguished in law," her hostess, Serena Fisk, had told her vaguely. "Not a judge, but a rather famous defending counsel, or prosecuting counsel, or *something* of that sort."

He had been rather quiet as they all sat down: urbane, courteous in a dated sort of way, but quiet. It was as if he was far away, reviewing the finer points of a case long ago.

"So nice to have *soup*," said Marcia, famous for "drawing people out," especially men. "Soup seems almost to have gone out these days."

"Really?" said Sir James, as if they were discussing the habits of Eskimos or Trobriand Islanders. "Yes, I suppose you don't often . . . *get it*."

"No, it's all melons and ham, and pâté, and antipasto."

"Is it? *Is* it?"

His concentration wavering, he returned to his soup, which he was consuming a good deal more expertly than Marcia, who, truth to tell, was more used to melons and suchlike.

"You don't eat out a great deal?"

"No. Not now. Once, when I was practicing. . . . But not now. And not since my wife died."

"Of course you're right: people don't like singles, do they?"

"Singles?"

"People on their own. For dinner parties. They have to find another one—like me tonight."

"Yes. . . . Yes," he said, as if only half understanding what she said.

"And it's no fun eating in a restaurant on your own, is it?"

"No. . . . None at all. . . . I have a woman come in," he added, as if trying to make a contribution of his own.

"To cook and clean for you?"

"Yes. . . . Perfectly capable woman. . . . It's not the same, though."

"No. Nothing is, is it, when you find yourself on your own?"

"No, it's not. . . ." He thought, as if thought was difficult. "You can't *do* so many things you used to do."

"Ah, you find that too, do you? What do you miss most?"

There was a moment's silence, as if he had forgotten what they were talking about. Then he said: "Travel. I'd like to go to the Lakes again."

"Oh, the Lakes! One of my favorite places. Don't you drive?"

"No. I've never had any need before."

"Do you have children?"

He had to think about that, really working at it, but coming up triumphant.

"Oh yes. Two sons. One in medicine, one in politics. Busy chaps with families of their own. Can't expect them to take me places. . . . Don't see much of them. . . ." His moment of animation seemed to fade, and he picked away at his entrée. "What *is* this fish, Molly?"

When the next day she phoned to thank her hostess, Marcia commented that Sir James was "such a sweetie."

"You and he seemed to get on like a house on fire, anyway."

"Oh, we did."

"Other people said he was awfully vague."

"Oh, it's the legal mind. Wrapped in grand generalities. His wife been dead long?"

"About two years. I believe he misses her frightfully. Molly used to arrange all the practicalities for him."

"I can believe that. I was supposed to ring him about a book I have that he wanted, but he forgot to give me his number."

"Oh, it's 271876. A rather grand place in Chelsea."

But Marcia had already guessed the number after going through the telephone directory. She had also guessed at the name of Sir James's late wife.

⊗

"We can't do much till we have the pathologist's report," said Superintendent Southern, fingering the still-damp material of a tweed suit. "Except perhaps about *this*."

Sergeant Potter looked down at it.

"I don't know a lot about such things," he said, "but I'd have said that suit was dear."

"So would I. A gentleman's suit, made to measure and beautifully sewn. I've had one of the secretaries in who knows about these things. A gentleman's suit for country wear. Made for a man who doesn't know the meaning of the word 'casual.' With a name tag sewn in by the tailor and crudely removed . . . with a razor blade probably."

"You don't *get* razor blades much these days."

"Perhaps he's also someone who doesn't know the meaning of the word 'throwaway.' A picture seems to be emerging."

"And the removal of the name tag almost inevitably means—"

"Murder. Yes, I'd say so."

✠

Marcia decided against ringing Sir James up. She felt sure he would not remember who she was. Instead she would call on him in Chelsea with the book, which had indeed come up in conversation—because she had made sure it did. Marcia was very good at fostering acquaintanceships with men, and had had two moderately lucrative divorces to prove it.

She timed her visit for late afternoon, when she calculated that the lady who cooked and "did" for him would have gone home. When he opened the door he blinked, and his hand strayed toward his lips.

"I'm afraid I—"

"Marcia Catchpole. We met at Serena Fisk's. I brought the book on Wordsworth we were talking about."

She proffered Stephen Gill on Wordsworth, in paperback. She had thought as she bought it that Sir James was probably not used to paperbacks, but she decided that, as an investment, Sir James was not yet worth the price of a hardback.

"Oh, I don't . . . er . . . Won't you come in?"

"Lovely!"

She was taken into a rather grim sitting room, lined with legal books and Victorian first editions. Sir James began to make uncertain remarks about how he thought he could manage tea.

"Why don't you let me make it? You'll not be used to fending for yourself, let alone for visitors. It was different in your generation, wasn't it? Is that the kitchen?"

And she immediately showed an uncanny instinct for finding things and doing the necessary. Sir James watched her bemused for a minute or two, as if wondering how she came to be so familiar with his kitchen, then shuffled back to the sitting room. When she came in with a tray, with tea things on it and a plate of biscuits, he looked as if he had forgotten who she was and how she came to be there.

"There, that's nice, isn't it? Do you like it strong? Not too strong, right? I think you'll enjoy the Wordsworth book. Wordsworth really *is* the Lakes, don't you agree?"

She had formed the notion, when talking to him at Serena Fisk's dinner party, that his reading was remaining with him longer than his grip on real life. This was confirmed by the conversation on this visit. As long as the talk stayed with Wordsworth and his Lakeland circle it approached a normal chat: he would forget the names of poems, but he would sometimes quote several lines of the better-known ones verbatim. Marcia had been educated at a moderately good state school, and she managed to keep her end up.

Marcia got up to go just at the right time, when Sir James had got used to her being there and before he began wanting her to go. At the door she said: "I'm expecting to have to go to the Lakes in a couple of weeks. On business. I'd be happy if you'd come along."

"Oh, I couldn't possibly—"

"No obligations either way: we pay for ourselves, separate rooms *of course,* quite independent of each other. My business is in Cockermouth, and I thought of staying by Buttermere or Crummock Water."

A glint came into his eyes.

"It would be wonderful to see them again. But I really couldn't—"

"Of course you could. It would be my pleasure. It's always better in congenial company, isn't it? I'll be in touch about the arrangements."

Marcia was in no doubt she would have to make all the

arrangements, down to doing his packing and contacting his cleaning woman. But she was confident she would bring it off.

✠

"Killed by a blow to the head," said Superintendent Southern, when he had skimmed through the pathologist's report. "Some kind of accident, for example a boating accident, can't entirely be ruled out, but there was some time between his being killed and his going into the water."

"In which case, what happened to the boat? And why didn't whoever was with him simply go back to base and report it, rather than heaving him out?"

"Exactly. . . . From what remains the pathologist suggests a smooth liver—a townie not a countryman, even of the upper-crust kind."

"I think you suspected that from the suit, didn't you, sir?"

"I did. Where do you go for a first-rate suit for country holidays if you're a townie?"

"Same as for business suits? Savile Row, sir?"

"If you're a well-heeled Londoner that's exactly where you go. We'll start there."

✠

Marcia went round to Sir James's two days before she had decided to set off North. Sir James remembered little or nothing about the proposed trip, still less whether he had agreed to go. Marcia got them a cup of tea, put maps on his lap, then began his packing for him. Before she went she cooked him a light supper (wondering how he had ever managed to cook for himself) and got out of him the name of his daily. Later on she rang her and told her she was taking Sir James to the Lakes, and he'd be away for at most a week. The woman sounded skeptical but uncertain whether it was her place to say anything. Marcia, in any case, didn't give her the opportunity. The woman's voice did not suggest she had any affection, or any great concern, for Sir James.

She also rang Serena Fisk to tell her. She had an ulterior motive for doing so. In the course of the conversation she casually asked: "How did he get to your dinner party?"

"Oh, I drove him. Homecooks were doing the food, so there was no problem. Those sons of his wouldn't lift a finger to help him. Then Bill drove him home later. Said he couldn't get a coherent word out of him."

"I expect he was tired. If you talk to him about literature you can see there's still a mind there."

"Literature was never my strong point, Marcia."

"Anyway, I'm taking him to the Lakes for a week on Friday."

"*Really?* Well, you are getting on well with him. Rather you than me."

"Oh, all he needs is a bit of stimulus," said Marcia brightly. She felt confident now that she had little to fear from old friends or sons.

This first visit to the Lakes went off extremely well from Marcia's point of view. When she collected him the idea that he was going somewhere seemed actually to have got through to him. She finished the packing with his toilet bag and other last-minute things, got him and his cases into the car and in no time they were on the M1. During a pub lunch he called her "Molly" again, and when they at last reached the Lakes she saw that glint in his eye, heard little grunts of pleasure.

She had booked them into Crummock Lodge, an unpretentious but spacious hotel which seemed to her just the sort of place Sir James would have been used to on his holidays in the Lakes. They had separate rooms, as she had promised. "He's an old friend who's been very ill," she told the manager. They ate well, went on drives and gentle walks. If anyone stopped and talked Sir James managed a sort of distant benignity which carried them through. As before, he was best if he talked about literature. Once, after Marcia had had a conversation with a farmer over a dry stone wall he said:

"Wordsworth always believed in the wisdom of simple country people."

It sounded like something a schoolmaster had once drummed into him. Marcia would have liked to say: "But when his brother married a servant he said it was an outrage." But she herself had risen by marriage, or marriages, and the point seemed to strike too close to home.

On the afternoon when she had her private business in Cockermouth she walked Sir James hard in the morning and left him tucked up in bed after lunch. Then she visited a friend who had retired to a small cottage on the outskirts of the town. He had been a private detective, and had been useful to her in her first divorce. The dicey method he had used to get dirt on her husband had convinced her that in his case private detection was very close to crime itself, and she had maintained the connection. She told him the outline of what she had in mind, and told him she might need him in the future.

When after a week they returned to London, Marcia was completely satisfied. She now had a secure place in Sir James's life. He no longer looked bewildered when she came round, even looked pleased, and frequently called her "Molly." She went to the Chelsea house often in the evenings, cooked his meal for him and together they watched television like an old couple.

It would soon be time to make arrangements at a Registry Office.

❈

In the process of walking from establishment to establishment in Savile Row, Southern came to feel he had had as much as he could stand of stiffness, professional discretion and awed hush. They were only high-class tailors, he thought to himself, not the Church of bloody England. Still, when they heard that one of their clients could have ended up as an anonymous corpse in Derwent Water they were willing to cooperate. The three establishments which offered that particular tweed handed him silently a list of those customers who had had suits made from it in the last ten years.

"Would you know if any of these are dead?" he asked one shop manager.

"Of course, sir. We make a note in our records when their obituary appears in *The Times*."

The man took the paper back and put a little crucifix sign against two of the four names. The two remaining were a well-known television newsreader and Sir James Harrington.

"Is Sir James still alive?"

"Oh, certainly. There's been no obituary for him. But he's very old: we have had no order from him for some time."

It was Sir James that Southern decided to start with. Scotland Yard knew all about him, and provided a picture, a review of the major trials in which he had featured and his address. When Southern failed to get an answer from phone calls to the house, he went round to try the personal touch. There was a FOR SALE notice on it that looked to have been there for some time.

✼

The arrangements for the Registry Office wedding went without a hitch. A month after their trip Marcia went to book it in a suburb where neither Sir James nor she was known. Then she began foreshadowing it to Sir James, to accustom him to the idea.

"Best make it legal," she said, in her slightly vulgar way.

"Legal?" he inquired, from a great distance.

"You and me. But we'll just go on as we are."

She thought about witnesses, foresaw various dangers from most of the possible ones in London and decided to pay for her detective friend to come down. He was the one person who knew of her intentions, and he could study Sir James's manner.

"Got a lady friend you could bring with you?" she asked when she rang him.

"Course I have. Though nobody as desirable as you, Marcia love."

"Keep your desires to yourself, Ben Brackett. This is business."

Sir James went through the ceremony with that generalized dignity which had characterized him in all his dealings with Marcia. He behaved to Ben Brackett and his lady friend as if they were somewhat dodgy witnesses who happened to be on his side in this particular trial. He spoke his words clearly, and almost seemed to mean them. Marcia told herself that in marrying her he was doing what he actually wanted to do. She didn't risk any celebration after the ceremony. She paid off Ben Brackett, drove Sir James home to change and pack again, then set off for the Lake District.

This time she had rented a cottage, as being more private. It was just outside Grange—a two-bedroom stone cottage, very comfortable and rather expensive. She had taken it for six weeks in the name of Sir James and Lady Harrington. Once there and settled in, Sir James seemed, in his way, vaguely happy: he would potter off on his own down to the lakeside, or up the narrow lanes abutting fields. He would raise his hat to villagers and tourists, and swap remarks about the weather.

He also signed, in a wavering hand, anything put in front of him.

Marcia wrote first to his sons, similar but not identical letters, telling them of his marriage and of his happiness with his dear wife. The letters also touched on business matters: "I wonder if you would object if I put the house on the market? After living up here I cannot imagine living in London again. Of course, the money would come to you after my wife's death." At the foot of Marcia's typed script Sir James wrote at her direction: "Your loving Dad."

The letters brought two furious responses, as Marcia had known they would. Both were addressed to her, and both threatened legal action. Both said they knew their father was mentally incapable of deciding to marry again, and accused her of taking advantage of his senility.

"My dear boys," typed Marcia gleefully. "I am surprised that you apparently consider me senile, and wonder how you could have allowed me to live alone without proper care if you believed that to be the case."

Back and forth the letters flew. Gradually Marcia discerned a subtle difference between the two sets of letters. Those from the MP were slightly less shrill, slightly more accommodating. He fears a scandal, she thought. Nothing worse than a messy court case for an MP's reputation. It was to Sir Evelyn Harrington, MP for Finchingford, that she made her proposal.

�֎

Southern found the estate agents quite obliging. Their dealings, they said, had been with Sir James himself. He had signed all the letters from Cumbria. They showed Southern the file, and he noted the shaky signature. Once they had spoken to Lady Harrington, they said: a low offer had been received, which demanded a quick decision. They had not recommended acceptance, since, though the property market was more dead than alive, a good house in Chelsea was bound to make a very handsome sum once it picked up. Lady Harrington had said that Sir James had a slight cold, but that he agreed with them that the offer was derisory and should be refused.

Southern's brow creased: wasn't Lady Harrington dead?

There was clearly enough of interest about Sir James Harrington to stay with him for a bit. Southern consulted the file at Scotland Yard and set up a meeting with the man's son at the House of Commons.

Sir Evelyn was in his late forties, tall and well set up. He had been knighted, Southern had discovered, in the last mass knighting of Tory backbenchers who had always voted at their party's call. The impression Sir Evelyn made was not of a stupid man, but of an unoriginal one.

"My father? Oh yes, he's alive. Living up in the Lake District somewhere."

"You're sure of this?"

"Sure as one can be when there's no contact." Southern left a silence, so the man was forced to elaborate. "Never was much. He's a remote bugger . . . a remote sort of chap, my father. Stiff, always working, never had the sort of common touch you need with children. Too keen on being the world's greatest prosecuting counsel. . . . He sent us away to school when we were seven."

Suddenly there was anger, pain and real humanity in the voice.

"You resented that?"

"*Yes.* My brother had gone the year before, and told me what that prep school was like. I pleaded with him. But he sent me just the same."

"Did your mother want you to go?"

"My mother did as she was told. Or else."

"That's not the present Lady Harrington?"

"Oh no. The present Lady Harrington is, I like to think, what my father deserves. . . . We'd been warned he was failing by his daily. Dinner burnt in the oven, forgetting to change his clothes, that kind of thing. We didn't take too much notice. The difficulties of getting a stiff-necked old . . . man into residential care seemed insuperable. Then the next we heard he'd married again and gone to live in the Lake District."

"Didn't you protest?"

"Of course we did. It was obvious she was after his money. And the letters he wrote, or she wrote for him, were all wrong. He would *never* have signed himself 'Dad,' let alone 'Your loving Dad.' But the kind of action that would have been necessary to annul the marriage can look ugly—for *both* sides of the case. So when she proposed an independent examination by a local doctor and psychiatrist I persuaded my brother to agree."

"And what did they say?"

"Said he was vague, a little forgetful, but perfectly capable of understanding what he'd done when he married her, and apparently very happy." He paused, his mouth set in an unforgiving line. "That was the end of the matter for us. The end of *him*."

❈

Marcia had decided from the beginning that in the early months of her life as Lady Harrington she and Sir James would have to move around a lot. As long as he was merely an elderly gentleman pottering around the Lakes and exchanging meteorological banalities with the locals there was little to fear. But as they became used to him there was a danger that they would try to engage him in conversation of more substance. If that happened his mental state might very quickly become apparent.

As negotiations with the two sons developed, Marcia began to see her way clear. Their six weeks at Grange were nearing an end, so she arranged to rent a cottage between Crummock Water and Cockermouth. When the sons agreed to an independent assessment of their father's mental condition and nominated a doctor and a psychiatrist from Keswick to undertake it, Marcia phoned them and arranged their visit for one of their first days in the new cottage. Then she booked Sir James and herself into Crummock Lodge for the relevant days. "I'll be busy getting the cottage ready," she told the manager. She felt distinctly pleased with herself. No danger of the independent team talking to locals.

"I don't see why we have to move," complained Sir James when she told him. "I like it here."

"Oh, we need to see a few places before we decide where we really want to settle," said Marcia soothingly. "I've booked us into Crummock Lodge, so I'll be able to get the new cottage looking nice before we move in."

"This is nice. I want to stay here."

There was no problem with money. On a drive to Cockermouth, Marcia had arranged to have Sir James's bank account transferred there. He had signed the form without a qualm, together with one making the account a joint one. Everything in the London house was put into store, and the estate agents forwarded Sir James's mail, including his dividend checks and his pension, regularly. There was no hurry about selling the house, but when it did finally go Marcia foresaw herself in clover. With Sir James, of course, and he was a bit of a bore. But very much worth putting up with.

As Marcia began discreetly packing for the move, Sir James's agitation grew, his complaints became more insistent.

"I don't want to move. Why should we move, Molly? We're happy here. If we can't have this cottage we can buy a place. There are houses for sale."

To take his mind off it Marcia borrowed their neighbor's rowing boat and took him for a little trip on the lake. It didn't take his mind off it. "This is lovely," he kept saying. "Derwent Water has always been my favorite. Why should we move on? I'm not moving, Molly."

He was beginning to get on her nerves. She had to tell herself that a few frazzled nerves were a small price to pay.

The night before they were due to move the packing had to be done openly. Marcia brought all the suitcases into the living room and began methodically distributing to each one the belongings they had brought with them. Sir James had been dozing when she began, as he often did in the evening. She was halfway through her task when she realized he was awake and struggling to his feet.

"You haven't been listening to what I've been saying, have you, Molly? Well, have you, woman? I'm not moving!"

Marcia got to her feet.

"I know it's upsetting, dear—"

"It's not upsetting, because we're staying here."

"Perhaps it will only be for a time. I've got it all organized, and you'll be quite comfy—"

"Don't treat me like a child, Molly!" Suddenly she realized with a shock that he had raised his arm. "Don't treat me like a child!" His hand came down with a feeble slap across her cheek. "Listen to what I say, woman!" Slap again. "I am not moving!" This time he punched her, and it hurt. "You'll do what I say, or it'll be the worse for you!" And he punched her again.

Marcia exploded with rage.

"You *bloody* old bully!" she screamed. "You brute! That's how you treated your wife, is it? Well, it's not how you're treating me!"

She brought up her stronger hands and gave him an almighty shove away from her even as he raised his fist for another punch. He lurched back, tried to regain his balance, then fell against the fireplace, hitting his head hard against the corner of the mantelpiece. Then he crumpled to the floor and lay still.

For a moment Marcia did nothing. Then she sat down and sobbed. She wasn't a sobbing woman, but she felt she had had a sudden revelation of what this man's—this old monster's—relations had been with his late wife. She felt a sudden, sharp compassion for the dead Molly. She had never for a moment suspected it. She no longer felt pity for him, if she ever had. She felt contempt.

She dragged herself wearily to her feet. She'd put him to bed, and by morning he'd have forgotten. She bent down over him. Then, panic-stricken, she put her hand to his mouth, felt his chest, felt for his heart. It didn't take long to tell that he was dead. She sat down on the sofa and contemplated the wreck of her plans.

❈

Southern and Potter found the woman in the general store-cum-newsagent's at Grange chatty and informative.

"Oh, Sir James. Yes, they were here for several weeks. Nice enough couple, though I think he'd married beneath him."

"Was he in full possession of his faculties, do you think?"

The woman hesitated.

"Well, you'd have thought so. Always said: 'Nice day,' or 'Hope the rain keeps off,' if he came in for a tin of tobacco or a bottle of wine. But no more than that. Then one day I said: 'Shame about the Waleses, isn't it?'—you know, at the time of the split-up. He seemed bewildered, and I thought he imagined I was talking about whaling or something, so I said: 'The Prince and Princess of Wales separating.' Even then it was obvious he didn't understand. It was embarrassing. I turned away and served somebody else. But there's others had the same experience."

After some minutes Marcia found it intolerable to be in the same room as the body. Trying to look the other way, she dragged it through to the dining room. Even as she did so she realized that she had made a decision: she was not going to the police, and her plans were not at an end.

Because after all she had her "Sir James" all lined up. In the operation planned for the next few days the existence of the real one was anyway something of an embarrassment. Now that stumbling block had been removed. She rang Ben Brackett and told him there had been a slight change of plan, but it needn't affect his part in it. She rang Crummock Lodge and told them that Sir James had changed his mind and wanted to settle straight into the new cottage. While there was still some dim light she went into the garden and out into the lonely land behind, collecting as many large stones as she could find. Then she slipped down and put them into the rowing boat she had borrowed from her neighbor the day before.

She had no illusions about the size—or more specifically the weight—of the problem she had in disposing of the body. She gave herself a stiff brandy, but no more than one. She found a razor blade and, shaking, removed the name from Sir James's suit. Then she finished her packing, so that everything was ready for departure. The farming people of the area were early to bed as a rule, but there were too many tourists staying there, she calculated, for it to be really safe before the early hours. At precisely one o'clock she began the long haul down to the shore. Sir James had been nearly six foot, so though his form was wasted he was both heavy and difficult to lift. Marcia found, though, that carrying was easier than dragging, and quieter too. In three arduous stages she got him to the boat, then into it. The worst was over. She rowed out to the dark center of the lake—the crescent moon was blessedly obscured by clouds—filled his pockets with stones, then carefully, gradually, eased the body out of the boat and into the water. She watched it sink, then made for the shore. Two large brandies later she piled the cases into the car, locked up the cottage and drove off in the Cockermouth direction.

Once the horror and difficulty of the night were over, everything went beautifully. Marcia had barely settled into the new cottage when Ben Brackett arrived. He already had some of Sir James's characteristics off pat: his distant, condescending affability, for example. Marcia coached him in others, and they tried to marry them to qualities the real Sir James had no longer had: lucidity and purpose.

When the team of two arrived, the fake Sir James was

working in the garden. "Got to get it in some sort of order," he explained, in his upper-class voice. "Haven't the strength I once had, though." When they were all inside, and over a splendid afternoon tea, he paid eloquent tribute to his new wife.

"She's made a new man of me," he explained. "I was letting myself go after Molly died. Marcia pulled me up in my tracks and brought me round. Oh, I know the boys are angry. I don't blame them. In fact, I blame myself. I was never a good father to them—too busy to be one. Got my priorities wrong. But it won't hurt them to wait a few more years for the money."

The team was clearly impressed. They steered the talk round to politics, the international situation, changes in the law. "Sir James" kept his end up, all in that rather grand voice and distant manner. When the two men left, Marcia knew that her problems were over. She and Ben Brackett waited for the sound of the car leaving to go back to Keswick, then she poured very large whiskies for them. Over their third she told him what had happened to the real Sir James.

"You did superbly," said Ben Brackett when she had finished.

"It was bloody difficult."

"I bet it was. But it was worth it. Look how it went today. A piece of cake. We had them in the palms of our hands. We won, Marcia! Let's have another drink on that. We won!"

Even as she poured Marcia registered disquiet at that "we."

Sitting in the superintendent's poky office in Kendal, Southern and Potter surveyed the reports and all the other pieces of evidence they had set out on the desk.

"It's becoming quite clear," said Southern thoughtfully. "In Grange we have an old man who hardly seems to know who the Prince and Princess of Wales are. In the cottage near Cockermouth we have an old man who can talk confidently about politics and the law. In Grange we have a feeble man, and a corpse which is that of a soft liver. In the other cottage we have a man who gardens—perhaps to justify the fact that his hands are *not* those of a soft-living lawyer. At some time between taking her husband on the lake—was that a rehearsal, I wonder?—and the departure in the night, she killed him. She must already have had someone lined up to take his place for the visit of the medical team."

"And they're there still," said Potter, pointing to the letter from the estate agents in London. "That's where all communications still go."

"And that's where we're going to go," said Southern, getting up.

They had got good information on the cottage from the Cockermouth police. They left their car in the car park of a roadside pub, and took the lane through fields and down toward the northern shore of Crummock Water. They soon saw the cottage, overlooking the lake, lonely. . . .

But the cottage was not as quiet as its surroundings. As they walked toward the place, they heard shouting. A minute or two later they heard two thick voices, arguing. When they could distinguish words it was in voices far from upper-crust:

"Will you get that drink, you cow? . . . How can I when I can hardly stand? . . . Get me that drink or it'll be the worse for you tomorrow. . . . You'd better remember who stands between you and a long jail sentence, Marcia. You'd do well to think about that *all the time.* . . . Now get me that scotch or you'll feel my fist!"

When Southern banged on the door there was silence. The woman who opened the door was haggard-looking, with bleary eyes and a bruise on the side of her face. In the room behind her, slumped back in a chair, they saw a man whose expensive clothes were in disarray, whose face was red and puffy and who most resembled a music-hall comic's version of a gentleman.

"Lady Harrington? I'm Superintendent Southern and this is Sergeant Potter. I wonder if we could come in? We have to talk to you."

He raised his ID toward her clouded eyes. She looked down at it slowly. When she looked up again Southern could have sworn that the expression on her face was one of relief.

Dog Television

The cat flap was a success from the start. For the first week or two the Perspex door was secured up, and Gummidge was convinced that this hole in the door was God-sent, and a secret known only to her: she used to look round to see if anyone was watching before jumping through it, preening herself on the other side that her secret was still safe. When the flap was let down she was suspicious and resentful at first, but she soon learned to pat it with her paw, like a boxer being playful, and to march through. Now her attitude to it changed: this is for ME, she seemed to say. It is MINE, and MINE ALONE. She looked with pity at Jaggers. If he had had a flap of his own it would take out a quarter of the door. So much better to have the petiteness and delicacy of a cat.

But in fact the cat flap was a godsend to Jaggers too. He began to sit on the doormat, his head on his paws, gazing through the Perspex at the human, animal and ornithological cavalcade which changed minute by minute, making the back garden a fascinating, endless soap opera: garbagemen came, and postmen, both to be barked at; birds swooped down on the bread crumbs left out for them, fought each other endlessly over the nut holder, dive-bombed the rough vegetable patch and bore off worms; male cats came in search of Gummidge, who was on the pill but still retained vestiges of her old attractions. There was always something going on. It was like one of those endless wildlife programs on television.

And in this case the screen image could literally leap into your living room. One day when Jaggers was not on sentry duty a tom leapt through the flap in search of Gummidge. Then there was mayhem. Peter was not at home, so the pursuit went on, with barks and feline shrieks for all of half an hour, before the tom, more by accident than by design, found his way out of the flap again. When Peter got home from school he found the living room so impregnated with tomcat smells that no amount of open windows or deodorant sprays could make it livable-in for days.

The flap was wonderful for inspecting callers too. This was the North, and the front door was for "special" callers, the back door for everyday. Jaggers could crouch and size up the dark blue trousers of gas or electricity meter readers, the bare legs of children wanting to be sponsored for this or that, or singing carols at Christmas, the varying garb of political canvassers. All were barked at, but the barks were subtly graded, from the downright menacing for garbagemen to the joyful welcoming for children.

Was it a child, that evening in March? The legs were bare and thin, and rather dirty too, and the skirt was above the knees. Still, the heels of her shoes were higher than children wore, except in play. Jaggers barked on, a middle-of-the-road, could-go-either-way kind of bark. Anyway, the ring of the door got Peter up from the pile of exercise books that he was marking in the front room to open the door.

"Oh, hello," he said. Friendly—yet somehow guarded. Jaggers wagged his tail tentatively.

"Hello again. Long time no see."

The tone of the visitor was cheeky, with an undertone of aggression. Jaggers recognized it. There was a Jack Russell that came to the park who took exactly that tone. It tended to run around, barking and snapping. This girl—woman—just stood there with her hands on her hips. Jaggers couldn't see her face, but he always judged more on body than on face.

"Come on in," said Peter.

They went through to the living room. Jaggers had realized by now that he had smelt the girl before. Not recently, but many seasons ago, when she had really been a child. Now she was dirtier, smelt stronger and better, but it was still the same human person. He wagged his tail and got a pat, but no more acknowledgment. The woman sat on the sofa, waiflike but not weak, not begging. The aggressive stance was still there, hardly hidden by any social veneer.

"I'll make a pot of tea," said Peter.

"Haven't you got anything stronger?"

Jaggers's master paused for thought.

"I've got a bottle of beer. . . . Oh yes, and there's still some gin left over from Christmas."

"Gin then. With whatever you've got."

Social gestures, then, were being made, however reluctantly. Enough for a tentative welcome. Jaggers wagged his tail— *thump,* and then *thump* again. He was rewarded by a caress of his ears, which was an acknowledgment of his presence that always delighted him. She wasn't a bad girl. He remembered that she had caressed him often, those times she had come before. Peter had liked her too. They had gone upstairs together.

Peter came back with the gin, and a little bottle of ginger ale. He put it down on the occasional table beside the sofa. She raised her eyebrows at the single glass, but Peter shook his head. He wasn't having anything, didn't want to make that social gesture. He sat tensely in his chair and waited. The girl-woman filled her glass from the bottle and drank half of it down. Then she slapped the glass down loudly on the table.

"You put me where I am now," she said.

"Where are you now?"

"On the streets."

"I did nothing of the sort."

Jaggers, his nose on the carpet under the table, was exploring her feet, delicately. They certainly were like no feet he had ever known before. He had known and appreciated Peter's feet after he had come back from a walk across the Pennines, or after a strenuous game of rugby, but these were different—or, rather, *more so*. Much, much dirtier. Layer upon layer of dirt—a dirt that extended, less concentrated, up her legs. It was on the feet that weeks, months, of living outside, living rough, showed most tellingly. Jaggers thought they were wonderful.

"It started upstairs here. It was my first time."

"You were as eager as any girl I've known."

"What kind of schoolteacher is it that takes his pupils to bed?"

"What kind of schoolkid is it who drags her teacher upstairs to bed? A slut, that's the answer. You were determined to be a slut."

"I'm on the streets. I'm not on the game."

The voices were getting raised. Jaggers no longer thumped his tail. He removed his head from under the table, to be ready if anything happened. The girl was shouting, accusing. She could attack Peter, throw herself at him. It had happened before, with other women.

There was a lull. The girl began jiggling her empty glass on the table. Peter sighed, got up and took it for a refill. Jaggers experimentally licked the feet, but got no answering caress. He lay there, unhappy at the situation.

"I want money."

"You'll have a job—getting money out of a schoolteacher!"

"You inherited this house—you told me. You can raise money on it."

"I've no intention of doing so."

"I'll take a hundred pounds."

"You won't. A hundred would only be a start."

"It might. But if I don't get it I'm going to your headmaster. If he doesn't listen I'll go to the press. And if they don't listen I'll go to the police."

The row didn't get any louder, but it got more intense. They somehow shouted at each other in voices that were hardly raised above a whisper. Jaggers found it unsettling, challenging to his role as defender of the house and its master. Peter was getting red in the face, and the girl was too, and her voice kept breaking as if she was going to sob. Eventually she shouted:

"What's a girl have to do to get a drink in this dump?"

When Peter went for her second refill Jaggers made a mistake. He looked at the girl to see that all was well, and then went to check up on the cat flap. It was a good hour since he had barked at those dirty legs. Dark had come, and there had been no birds around for hours. Now there was only the odd luminous eye of a tomcat, on the prowl in hopes of an amorous encounter with Gummidge.

When he had done his couple of minutes on sentry-go, he went back into the hall and found the living-room door shut.

Jaggers was unhappy. He had gone to fulfill one duty, and now found himself shut out from fulfilling another. He could not protect Peter now, nor even provide distraction. He lay with his nose against the bottom of the door, his tail quiet. Of the voices he could now hear no more than their rise and fall, the hiss of accusation, the suppressed fury of Peter's angry retorts. Surely soon he'd come out again?

But he didn't, and the curve of the voices became a continual rising one, not in volume but in intensity. Jaggers heard chair springs go—they were no longer sitting, but were confronting each other standing up. The curve continued upwards, the girl's voice like a whiplash with words of scorn and accusation. Jaggers was considering barking when he heard a tremendous thump, a shattering of glass, and then another bump—to the floor, on the other side of the room to the door. Then silence.

Jaggers whined, unhappy. Glass—he knew the sound of breaking glass. But what he'd heard wasn't like a breaking wineglass; it was something heavy, thick. . . . The thick gray glass ashtray, which had sat on the mantelpiece since Peter had given up smoking.

Still silence. Jagger's nose was firmly inserted into the tiny crack along the bottom of the door, as if by smell alone he could understand what was going on. He was just thinking that he might understand when Peter came out the door and shut it firmly behind him, then leaned his head against the doorjamb, sobbing.

The brief moment that the door was open had told Jaggers. It had given him the whiff of something he came across now and then in his walks in woods and moorlands, a phenomenon that was sometimes exciting, sometimes disconcerting. It was a Not-Being. An End to Being. Lying there without Being.

He went to the front door, whining, and lay there on the doormat. He no longer wanted to be near the living room.

Peter stood by the door, still sobbing, otherwise motionless, for some minutes. Then he went upstairs. Jaggers heard the lavatory flush, then water running in the bathroom. When he came down he was looking more normal, but Jaggers could tell from the way he came down the stairs that he was still tense. He looked in the mirror in the hall, to see that he did look normal. Then he fetched Jaggers's lead from the kitchen.

A walk at this hour! Unheard of! He jumped, frisked and barked—more than usually beside himself because he was happy to get out of the house. The air outside was fresh and . . . free from that blight that was now pervading indoors. They walked to the Jug and Bottle, and Peter took him into the saloon bar.

"Have you got such a thing as a bottle of whisky I could buy? And I'll have a half of bitter while I'm waiting."

Jaggers curled up contentedly by the brass rail around the floor of the bar. He saw no need to behave other than ordinarily.

"Having a party?" asked the landlord when he came back from the cellar.

"Not really. An old rugby friend rang up—may drop in later. Likes a drop of scotch."

"Show me a rugby player who doesn't," said the landlord. "When they've tanked up on beer."

On the way back Jaggers showed signs of reluctance. He didn't want to go back to the house. But where else was there to go? Peter let them in by the front door, then shut Jaggers and the whisky in the dining room. Jaggers sat listening. Peter didn't go into the sitting room. He went to the kitchen and soon returned with a jug of water and a glass. He poured whisky, then water, then sat at the table drinking. Jaggers sat close, watching him, waiting for some sign, some revelation of intention. Occasionally he wagged his tail, occasionally a hand would come down and caress his head. He was still unsettled. It was a comfort.

It was well after midnight, when the whisky bottle was a third empty, when Peter made a move. He got up, only a little unsteady, and left the room. Shutting the door behind him. Jaggers sat by the door, straining his ears. The house was surrounded by a tremendous night silence. Peter opened the back door, leaving it open, and Jaggers heard his steps go to the garden shed. Something taken from it—two heavy implements that clanged when he let them come together.

He was going to the vegetable plot—that large oval that he turned over every year, but somehow never seemed to do very much with. Jaggers jumped up against the bookshelf under the back window, peering into the darkness. Yes—he was forking over and then digging. He was in condition—he kept himself in condition. Jaggers lay down on the floor again, waiting.

After what seemed like an eternity Peter came back into the house. He came back into the dining room, chucking Jaggers's ears. Then he went to the whisky bottle, pouring himself a stiff one. He took his time drinking it: getting his breath or summoning up courage. Then he went out, shutting the door. Jaggers heard the sitting-room door being opened. That was where the Not Being thing was. He heard something heavy being dragged. That would be it. Little clinks as bits of glass knocked together on the floor. Peter dragged it into the hall. It seemed heavier than he had expected, or perhaps now he was tired. He had difficulty dragging it round from the sitting room through to the kitchen and the back door. He bumped into the dining-room door and it came off the latch. Jaggers watched, giving the tiniest thump of his tail, but did nothing.

The unmistakable sound of the back door being closed. In a second Jaggers was up and nosing at the dining-room door.

That was the first trick in the book. A moment and he was through it, and on his haunches in front of the cat flap, on duty again.

Peter had something in his arms. It. By the time he got to the vegetable patch they were nothing but shapes, but Jaggers could see that Peter had put It down. There was another, a new shape there. A mound. That must be It. A mound of earth. There were tiny, distant sounds. More digging. Peter had found he needed more digging. Then Jaggers saw the shape of Peter come round the mound, take up It, then lay It down, right in the hole.

Again he saw Peter come round the mound, spade in hand. He stood by the mound, and using the spade with strong, practiced motions, he began rapidly filling the hole. Shovelful followed shovelful, the man powered by alcohol and desperation. In ten minutes the mound was nearly flattened again.

In the kitchen Jaggers still kept watch. His tail went thump, thump, thump regularly on the linoed floor. His mind was on the future.

What had been buried cried out to be dug up again.

The Women
at the Funeral

Alice Furnley closed her brother's eyes and turned to her sisters.

"He'll be in heaven now," she said.

The two younger sisters nodded. There was no doubt about that. They went into the next bedroom to tell their mother, who had been expecting it.

"If only I could have gone first," she said, tears running down her wrinkled cheeks. "But there—it's God's will. He'll be one more saint in the holy choir."

They all murmured their assent, without hesitation or reservation. They knew their brother Roderick had been a man of singular gentleness and boundless charity. His consideration for his old mother and his sisters was much commended in the parish: the old lady was eighty-two, and very frail; two of his sisters were spinsters and the other had been early widowed. They all lived together in the large house and grounds in Acacia Avenue, in great harmony. "We never had an unkind word from him," Alice told the vicar, who had prayed for him the previous Sunday at St. Michael's. He had described Roderick as a man of boundless goodness and of good works, an example to them all. His sisters, in the family pew, had nodded. They were women of faith, of certainties, and their minds were not inquiring ones.

Alice's first uneasiness came at the funeral service, or

rather just after it. There had been many tears shed during the address and the prayers, for a number of the congregation at St. Michael's, not just his sisters, felt they had lost a brother: he had been counselor and confessor to many of them, had given solid aid to more than a few. The vicar had meditated, to no very good effect, on the ways of God, particularly in taking to himself so admirable a man at the early age of fifty-two. As the coffin was borne down the aisle and out to the churchyard for burial the congregation held back to allow the mourning women of the family to follow it. Sarah and Emily, the two younger sisters, helped their mother along, and were preoccupied, but Alice could look around her, could see that the church was three-quarters full, and, as she came to the pews at the back, could get a good view of the unknown women.

They were sitting together, nine or ten of them, and they were clearly uncertain what to do at a funeral, or even in church. They had gone to some effort to make their dresses appropriate to the occasion: black or brown skirts, little dark hats or head scarves. But they were not at all the class of women that Alice would have expected at her brother's funeral, and they were not—Alice found it difficult to find a way of putting it to herself—they were not, they didn't *look*, respectable. She went out into the bitter December wind.

There was no question of celebrating Christmas that year. Most of the customary seasonal indulgences were canceled, and those that could not be were consumed soberly, often with sad comment about how much Roderick had always enjoyed this or that. Alice said nothing to her sisters about the women in the church, but she felt weighed down by her secret. On Boxing Day the tradespeople and roundsmen were tipped by Alice, through Cook, with particular generosity, which she felt her brother would have expected. It was on that day, in the late afternoon, that she had a visitor.

Mary, the little maid, quite new from one of Dr. Barnardo's establishments, looked more than a little confused.

"Wouldn't give no name, miss, said it wouldn't mean anything to you. But she asked special to speak to you alone, miss. She's not—"

"Not what, Mary?"

"Not—not like one of us. Not a lady, miss."

And that, in the year of 1891, presented a problem. *Where* was this talk to take place? Not in the drawing room, surely, especially as one of her sisters might come in at any time.

"Show her into Mr. Roderick's study," Alice said. "And tell my sisters I am busy."

Alice was not new to taking household decisions, but this one was unexpected, outside her usual scope. She felt almost nervous as she waited in the study. When the young woman was shown in she knew at once it must be one of the ones she had seen at the back of the church: she had on the same sort of dull, dun clothes and the same look of cleanliness achieved with effort. Now, as then, the visitor was not at ease.

"I thought as how I should come, Miss Furnley," she said, from just inside the door, "in case you was worried or upset about the will."

"The will? My brother's will?" Alice heard uneasiness in her voice and repressed it firmly. "We have had no time to see the family solicitor as yet. Christmas, you understand. . . ."

The woman bit her lip.

"Oh, I see. Well, I'm glad, miss, because you might have wondered. . . ."

"Wondered?"

"Oh, no need to be uneasy, miss."

Alice drew herself up.

"I am not uneasy. Merely bewildered what my brother's will could have to do with you."

"O' course, miss. Well, you see, he told me as how he was going to leave me something. Oh, not a great sum. Something you could easily afford."

"I see." But it was said faintly, and Alice Furnley clearly did not see.

"And o' course it's not for me, not for myself."

"He left you money, but not for yourself?"

"That's right, miss. It's because he knew he could trust me, and because I know a bit about banks and accounts and that. It's for me to keep, to help any of us girls."

"Any . . . of . . . you . . . girls," said Alice, more faintly still.

"If we're in trouble," said the woman, growing almost confiding. "In the nature o' things a lot of us get into trouble from time to time."

"You do?"

"Us being independent girls, working on our own, on the streets a lot. . . . There's a lot of rough men around in Leeds, you know, miss."

Alice looked at the carpet.

"I know *that*. I see them."

"That's all you want to do, miss. Anyway, there's lots of us girls have been helped over a bad patch by your brother—when we've been swindled, or beaten up, or put in 'orspital—that's when they'll take us in there. And he knew, when he was beginning to feel poorly, that if he left the money to me I'd keep it and give it or lend it as the need arose."

"I see." Alice began walking up and down the little room

to get a better look at the woman. She did indeed look honest. Rough but honest. "Let me get this right: my brother has left you a sum of money—"

"A thousand pounds."

"A thousand pounds!" Alice couldn't keep the surprise out of her voice. "My brother has left this sum to you so that you may relieve the distress of your . . . sisters."

"My friends, like. He didn't trust the churches and organizations. He said there was always strings attached."

"That sounds like Roderick." Alice was getting her confidence back. That did sound like Roderick. He was always direct and warm in his charities. This must be one he preferred—perhaps naturally—not to tell his womenfolk about. "He was so generous," she said. "So open."

"Oh, he was! Is this his room?" The woman looked around the book-lined little office, with copies of old *Punch*es, pipes and boots, and a chessboard by the fire. "I can imagine him in it. We all worshiped him!"

"All?"

"All the girls he was kind to. He never gave a lecture with it, that was the great thing, and you knew he was there in need."

"That's true."

"And he was always very considerate and gentle in—you know, in personal things."

Alice could not begin to think what she meant, so she stayed silent.

"Oh, you mustn't think badly of him," said the woman hurriedly. "All he wanted was a bit of comfort, a bit of relaxation, like." Seeing the bewilderment, then the horror, on Alice's face, she turned to go. "I won't take up any more of your time. Oh—just one more thing. That business with Mr.

Johnston. He told me he was going to tell you about that, and I'm the only other one who knows. I swear to God it'll go no further. The man's quite safe as far as I'm concerned, and always will be."

And she marched from the room, showing herself out through the front door. Alice watched her safely to the end of Acacia Avenue, then sank exhausted into a chair. What had she meant—*comfort? Relaxation?* Just when she had reconciled herself in her mind to the idea that Roderick had quietly been dispensing charity to women who . . . to *fallen* women (that must, surely, be what this woman had implied), there came this new revelation: that he had gone to this woman—these women—for comfort and relaxation. What could that mean except . . . ? Impossible to believe!

Yet even as she told herself that, Alice remembered those late evenings of Roderick's at the Liberal Club twice a week. And remembered too that her brother had never felt the need to be particularly active in the party cause at election time, nor had he ever shown great familiarity with the Liberal candidate, or even with party officials when he met them.

Alice took the decision to go to the family solicitor next day, and take only her sister Sarah—her once-married sister—with her. When the main provisions of the will were read, the division of the estate into three equal portions for his sisters, the two women nodded: they had known that was what Roderick had intended. When the will said that the deceased trusted his dear sisters' generosity to give adequate remembrances of himself to the family's servants and dependents, Alice whispered: "We must give them something they'll be *very* pleased with." And when one thousand pounds was left to Mrs. Sally Hardwick, of Crow Lane, Armley, Alice whispered: "One of those poor people Roderick was always so kind to—large family, father dead." If Sarah Furnley thought that one thousand pounds was an awful lot of money to leave a poor family, even a fatherless one, she said nothing: it would have been unseemly, almost blasphemous, to question Roderick's judgment.

The next day Alice went to the bank and on her return gave seventy-five pounds to Cook, fifty pounds to the ladies' maid, the same to Frank the gardener, and ten pounds to little Mary, with strict instructions to save most of it against the time a respectable young man asked her to marry him.

Which left Alice with the problem of Mr. Johnston. What on earth could the woman—could Sally Hardwick—have meant? The Furnleys had no close friends called Johnston. Racking her brains, Alice could recall that there was a Mr. Johnston among the congregation at St. Michael's. He was a bachelor and an elderly man, almost as old as their mother. Surely there could be no secret concerning him that Roderick had kept? She looked in trade directories, asked Walter Wakeham, who now ran the family clothing manufactory, if he knew of a Mr. Johnston that her brother Roderick was close to. All to no avail. It was a blank wall. When she decided that the woman could have got it wrong, or she had misheard, and it was a Mr. *Johnson* who was meant, her perplexity increased. There were just too many Johnsons around—and even so, no family or man of that name with whom the Furnleys had been close.

It seemed like an unsolvable puzzle. Alice could think of nothing more she could do, short of employing a private detective. But that was all but unthinkable: she had the impression that these were most unsavory individuals who would not scruple to use any discreditable information they found out against their employer, so she put that possibility from her mind. Though she acknowledged to herself her own helplessness, she found that the name Johnston jumped out at her from the pages of the *Leeds Advertiser* or the *Yorkshire Post* in the way that names one is interested in have a habit of doing (other names which thus leapt off the page for Alice Furnley were the Prince of Wales and Marie Corelli, whose novels she found painfully exciting).

But it was not from the pages of a newspaper that the name of the Johnston she had been looking for sprang at her. She was sitting in the family pew at St. Michael's in early autumn, praying for her mother, whose life was drawing to a sad close, and the vicar was reading the banns of marriage:

"Francis Johnston, bachelor of this parish, to Ellen Currey, spinster of this parish . . ."

Alice had started involuntarily at the name and looked round. Her sister Emily smiled and patted her arm. "Frank," she said. "Isn't it nice?" Alice nodded and subsided into her pew.

Frank the gardener. She knew he had got engaged to a girl—no, to a woman—who worked for old Mrs. Macklin round the corner in Galton Road. She'd heard the name Ellen—that was why several bells had rung when the banns were read. Because she had never to her knowledge heard Frank's surname: he had always been Frank to her, and nothing more. She might, if she racked her brain, remember little Mary's surname (probably a gift of the good Dr. Barnardo): but Frank was outdoor staff, and as such she had had in her brother's lifetime little to do with him beyond an occasional commending of his diligence or the excellence of his brussels sprouts.

It was three days before Alice had matured a plan of action in her mind. Sarah was shopping in Leeds and Emily was nursing their mother when she ventured into the long, leafy garden that stretched from the back of the house. Frank was busy separating daffodil bulbs and she approached him circuitously, collecting a little bunch of autumn flowers in a basket. As she drew near him he straightened himself respectfully. He was about middle height and capable-looking, but with strongly etched lines on his face that gave him an unhappy air.

"I was so glad to hear the banns read for you, Frank," Alice said.

"Thank you very much, miss."

"You must be looking forward to a happier time ahead."

There was a tiny pause before Frank said: "I am that."

"Because you've had a lot of trouble in the past, haven't you?"

This time there was a quite measurable pause before Frank said: "Did Mr. Roderick tell you about that? He said he was going to when he . . . took me on, then he changed his mind. Said he thought it would worry you, and you wouldn't understand."

"Before he died he told me," lied Alice, mentally excusing herself by her *need* to know. "He thought it was his duty, you see, as we would be left alone."

"I see, miss. I'm sure Mr. Roderick would always do what was right."

"But it was a very brief account—him being so weak. I didn't really understand the *circumstances* of your . . . problem."

"It must have sounded bad enough, miss, without the circumstances." Frank drew his sleeve across his forehead, which was beaded with sweat. "And it *was* bad, I acknowledge that freely. We were farm workers, you see, from down Lincolnshire way, me and my wife." Alice tried not to let it show that she was surprised he had had a wife, having been proclaimed a bachelor in her own church. "We were never well off, but when this depression hit the farmers we got poorer and poorer, hungrier and hungrier. I was just about to leave, to try and find work in the town, when it happened."

He looked at her as if hoping that she would supply the words he didn't want to say. Alice could only nod.

"First the boy, then the little girl—the light of my life. I won't say they died of hunger, not right out, but they were powerful weak when the influenza struck. We'd been going to lose our cottage the week after, but the farmer gave us another month, out of compassion. My poor wife was mad wi' grief, tearing her hair, miss, and crying from noon to night. As the time came for us to lose our home she kept saying: 'I don't want to live' and 'There's nothing left to live for.' And—to cut a long story short—we came to a sort of agreement."

"A suicide pact," whispered Alice, stunned by the wickedness of the idea.

"That's what they called it in court. We didn't have the words for it, not being educated people. I was willing, miss— didn't take no persuading. I had nothing to live for either. We went down to a little coppice, I wi' my gun, we kissed for the last time, and I shot her. It were like putting an animal out of its misery. I were just seeing that she was really dead, not going to come round, when the farmer ran up, wrestled the gun from me, and forced me back to the farm. I pleaded with him to let things take their course, but he locked me up and fetched the authorities."

"But you were not . . . ?" Alice began faintly.

"Hanged? No, miss. That were the sentence, but it was commuted. Maybe it'd have been better for all if it had been carried out. I got fifteen years' hard labor, and if my life had been hell before—pardon my language, miss—it was double hell in jail. I served three years, and if I could have ended my life I would have done it. They made sure I couldn't. But I got away while I was in prison in York—escaped from a working party. It's easier if you don't care if they shoot you or not."

"But how did my brother come to know about you?"

He twisted the cap which he was holding in his hand.

"That was through a . . . lady I knew and he knew. She told him my story, and he offered me this job. He was a saint, your brother, miss."

Alice made noises that she hoped sounded like assent. Once it would have been spontaneous, full-hearted agreement.

"I had my own contacts by then. I gave myself a new name, and got a birth certificate to prove it. I can never forget my poor wife, and my lovely children, but now I've got the chance of a new life. I'm very fond of Ellen, and I mean to take it."

"Yes. Yes, of course. Thank you for telling me all this. I wish you luck in the future."

And Alice made her way back to the house more directly than she had come from it. She went straight to her bedroom, sat by the little fire there, and tried to compose her thoughts. Her overwhelming feeling was anger: her brother had introduced into the house a murderer—a dreadful man who had killed his own wife, served only part of his prison sentence, and was in effect a convict on the run. And now a household of women—and Roderick had always been the sickly one, had often said he would be the first to go—had been left through his lack of thought or consideration with a brutal killer whom they daily came into contact with. She had not been able to say so to Johnston, for she would not have brought out into the open a disagreement with her late brother, but she thought it was *wicked.* It was contempt of the law, it was endangering his own family, it was condoning the sin of suicide. She could never, ever, think well of her brother again.

Meanwhile there was daily life to be got through, and a decision to be made about that. That decision bothered Alice sorely. She could hardly give Johnston up to the law, which was her first instinct: that would be to go against her brother's judgment totally and publicly, and she had always deferred to him as the eldest and as the head of the house. It would also destroy his reputation in the community by revealing the shaming fact that he had connived in defeating the proper workings of justice.

And yet, to have the man *there*, working around the house, to see him every day, a man who had killed his own wife! Alice could hardly bear to go out into her own garden.

In the end it was Johnston who ended the awkward situation. He contrived to be in the front garden when she was coming home from a sewing bee at the vicarage a week after their conversation.

"Oh, Miss Furnley, could I have a word?"

"Well, er . . . I'm very busy . . . a *quick* one, Johnston."

"I can see, miss, that you're not happy about . . . what we spoke about. No reason why you should be. I should have told you when we were talking that before he died, when he knew the tuberculosis had come back, your brother talked to me, said he wanted me to be set up in a small way, so as to be independent. He gave me seven hundred and fifty pounds. Walked away when I tried to thank him. Well, there's a small market garden I've had my eye on, and I've managed to buy it with part of the money. My wife and I will be able to live off that, and I'll be out of your way, not in front of your eyes every time you look out of the window."

Alice was surprised at the perceptiveness of this rough

man, but of course she could not say so. She said: "I wish you well in the future then, Johnston, and I'll advertise on Saturday for a replacement."

And that, though it did not exactly solve the problem, made it much less pressing. She had other things to occupy her mind. Her old mother died before the next Christmas, and the daughters were left alone in the house. Sarah married for a second time, not wisely or well, and within five years was back again. The younger sisters died first, but Alice lived on and on, ramrod straight, sharp of eye.

She saw Johnston from time to time, sometimes with his wife, eventually with children. She nodded to him graciously, in a way that did not encourage the exchange of words. Johnston himself never attempted that. The only time they talked was when she was a very old lady, in her late eighties, still walking the streets of Leeds dispensing charity to the deserving poor and attending church as one of the dwindling congregation of St. Michael's. The slaughter of young men which was the Great War had happened, and so had the influenza epidemic, which had slaughtered less unfairly as to sex. It was in the middle of the gay twenties, which were not particularly gay in Leeds, that she came upon Johnston, now a bent man in his seventies, with a bright, forceful young man, walking down Boar Lane. On an impulse she stopped.

"It's Johnston, isn't it?"

"That's right, Miss Furnley."

"And this is your son?"

"It is—Sam, our youngest."

"A prop for your old age. You are so fortunate. So many of my friends lost sons and grandsons in the war."

"I were just too young to serve, miss," said Sam. "Thank God."

"That's not a very patriotic sentiment," said Alice Furnley severely. "I sometimes think the dead were the lucky ones. 'They carried back bright to the coiner the mintage of man,' as the poet says. They never grew old and tarnished, as so often happens."

She looked meaningfully at Johnston. He stared doggedly back.

"If you mean your brother, miss, he went to his Maker as bright as any man ever did."

"Oh, come, Johnston, you know that's not true," she said, in a low voice, preparing to pass on. "You of all people know that."

And she marched on, determinedly continuing about her business.

"Silly old biddy," said young Sam. And for once his father did not reprove him.

PERFECT HONEYMOON

*B*y the time Carol reached her unspoiled Greek honeymoon island, she was beginning to wish it could have been just that tiny bit spoiled. After the ceremony, and the wedding breakfast with the speeches, there had been the drive off, the wait at Manchester airport, the night flight, the coach ride from the Athens airport, and now the long ferry trip to Mathos. As the island approached on the horizon, Carol was inclining to the view that an airstrip would have improved the place enormously.

Of course, David had been sweet through the entire trip. But then, knowing she had always been fascinated by the idea of Greece, this honeymoon trip had been his idea. So it was quite natural that he should keep her spirits up by little reminders of the romantic nature of the island, the exotic food, the excursions to Crete and Rhodes. And of course *the* pleasure of a honeymoon. David had always insisted that the first time would be in the luxury hotel on Mathos. David was old-fashioned. He didn't believe in anticipating marriage, and Carol thought it rather sweet of him. She had anticipated it all too often with other men.

Jutting up like a fairy cake in the middle of a brilliant blue tea cloth, Mathos assumed more definite shape.

"It's beautiful," said David. "Just perfect."

"It's all been just perfect," said Carol dreamily. "The wedding, the breakfast—everything."

"Almost perfect," responded David. "I just wish Dad could have been there to share it."

David had loved his father, who had died just before they had got engaged. He missed him, and found his new role as head of Lloyd-Johnson Agricultural Estates burdensome and worrying. Carol put her hand over his on the prow of the boat.

"Almost perfect," she agreed. "As perfect as we could make it."

As they neared the island, shapes began to appear. A ruined monastery on the hilltop, fishing boats and a pleasure yacht in the harbor, a restaurant with tables outside and red-checked tablecloths . . . people on the quayside.

"The local peasants, come to see us arrive," said David. "And a few tourists, I expect."

"We needn't talk to any of them if we don't want to," said Carol. "We have each other."

Suddenly, as the boat was approaching the quay, she was conscious of David's body stiffening.

"It can't be," he muttered. "It's just a . . . Oh, my *God!*"

His face was purple with rage. Carol had never seen him like that. He was such a gentle soul. She looked up at him with fear in her eyes.

"What is it, David?"

"The *swine*. The absolute swine. Don't you see who that is? It's that rotter Joshua Swayne."

"Oh, David, it *can't* be."

But it did look very like him indeed. He was standing at the end of the quay, just where the ferry was to dock. He was wearing beautifully tailored white trousers, and a dashing shirt open to the waist and knotted at the navel. He was very tanned, very fit-looking, so that even David's rural-proprietor complexion seemed beside his that of a country bumpkin. David, somehow, could never be said to look sexy.

"Take no notice of him," said David, red and furious. "He thinks we shall have to acknowledge him, standing there in the middle of the quay. Well, we don't have to. Walk right past him. Ignore him. My God, what a diabolical liberty! Who does he think he is?"

There was not much doubt who Joshua Swayne was. Less than a year ago his . . . wooing of Carol had been the talk of Merioneth, staple gossip in pubs and tearooms around the county. Joshua Swayne was only a greengrocer's son, but he certainly knew how to cut a dash. And Carol had always resisted that "only a greengrocer's son" formulation. Come to that, she was only a schoolteacher's daughter, wasn't she? Whatever else she was, she wasn't a snob. And if anyone asked her *how* he cut the dash that he did, what he did it *on,* she merely shrugged and said it was none of her business. He was just a very entertaining companion, she said. Oh yes? said everyone else.

"Just don't look at him," hissed David as the boat docked. "Walk off talking and don't acknowledge his existence. The cad!"

And that's what they did, though somehow it seemed terribly unnatural. They held hands, looked into each other's eyes, and walked straight past Joshua Swayne and on to the bus, where they sat, still talking in those unnaturally high voices, still looking anywhere but back to the quay, as the boot was loaded with their and the other tourists' luggage, and the bus began its steep ascent to the hotel.

Of course, when they got out and walked into the hotel lobby, there he was again. Somehow David had expected it, since the ride had been so short, and Joshua was a notable mountaineer—"the mountain goat" he had been called, somewhat ambiguously, at home. Half expecting it didn't make it any the easier for David to deal with. Carol went on ignoring him studiously, but as they marched up to the reception desk, and as he stood there in all his arrogant sexuality, David barked: "Get out of my way," and Joshua moved lithely aside with a pleasant smile. Somehow he always seemed to take the trick, however poor his cards.

They made their way to their room, watched from the open, sun-drenched doorway by Joshua, who seemed part, or product, of the sun itself. Once safely inside the bedroom, they sat on the bed and looked at each other.

"This is *dread*ful," said Carol. "Just unimaginable. He has no *right*."

"Of course he has no right. You threw him over for me, and there's an end of it."

"Actually I threw him over well *before* I got interested in you," Carol said. And indeed there had been all of a fortnight's gap between her breaking it off with Joshua and starting to go out with David. "He acts as though he owns me."

"I just can't see what's to be done."

"We could move to another hotel."

"And have him come after us? We'd become laughingstocks."

David was very conscious, always, of anybody laughing at him.

"But that means sticking it out here." Carol giggled shyly. "Of course, we could stay in our room the whole time, and that would be nice. But we have to have meals."

David looked around the room.

"We could. I suppose there must be room service. But I'm *damned* if I'm going to avoid the dining room because he'll be there."

"No. Why should we? Though it will be awkward. . . ."

David looked very glum.

"He's spoilt everything. You know, what I'd like to do now is . . . well . . . you know. But I just don't want it to happen in this sort of atmosphere. We've got to get this sorted out, one way or the other."

"Exactly. Because if we can't get it sorted out, we might as well go home and . . . start the marriage there." Carol looked at her watch. "Actually it's lunchtime now. And after all that traveling I *am* pretty hungry."

They both showered, separately and modestly, and then they put on clean summer clothes, crisp and delightful on the body, clothes in which David looked *almost* handsome, Carol thought, and definitely better than presentable. Then they went, holding hands, down to lunch.

He wasn't there when they went in, and for that they were grateful. But they had hardly stewed over the menu and given their orders to the waiter when they saw him come in the door from the foyer. The waiter tried to steer him to what was obviously his usual table, but they saw something pass from hand to hand, and he came over and sat himself at the next table.

"Good *morning*, again," he said cheerfully. "You really have picked well, you know. An inspired choice. Mathos could hardly be bettered for a honeymoon island. You're going to be awfully happy here."

David choked, and Carol managed a few reluctant murmurs of reply, for the benefit of other lunch-takers around them. Joshua had already turned to the waiter and began ordering in what sounded like idiomatic Greek, to a non-Greek. He might have been the cookery correspondent of a glossy magazine.

It was a ghastly meal. Everything they said could be heard by him at the next table. They scampered through their three courses, and as they were getting up, Joshua said:

"Enjoy the afternoon. There are some quite fabulous walks around here, you know. Just give me the nod any time you feel like it, and I'll show you round."

David and Carol choked with irritation. When they got to

the door David made a decision. He left Carol there and marched back down the dining room.

"Look here," he said, red-faced and bulgy-eyed, "just what is your game?"

Joshua raised his eyebrows and gave a cool smile up at him.

"Game, old man? I don't quite understand you. I'm here on holiday like yourselves—well, *almost* like yourselves."

"You're not going to tell me this is a coincidence."

"All right. I won't try and tell you this is a coincidence."

"You've come here deliberately, because you found out this was where we were coming."

"The island has many attractions," said Joshua, this time with a catlike smile. "And that, of course, was among them."

"If you think you're going to make us turn tail and flee, you'll be disappointed."

"On the contrary, I would be disappointed if you did. It would cause me so much hassle. But I know your sturdy Welsh stock, David, and I know you're not a quitter."

"I know you are a cad," David said, his voice rising, so that people began to look at him from tables quite far away, and he blushed and reduced it to a hiss again, "but I never thought you'd want to cause Carol this sort of distress."

"Is she distressed? I don't know why she should be. Most women like having two men at their beck and call."

"You are *not* at her beck and call."

"I certainly am, supposing she decides to beck or call."

"If you continue to force yourself on us in the way you have been doing today—"

"Yes?"

It was a thoroughly irritating question, and insolently delivered, the eyebrows raised quizzically. Because what, after all, could David threaten him with?

"I'll not answer for the consequences," David spluttered, and marched out of the dining room.

The consequences, unfortunately, were mostly on David's and Carol's heads. David said he really didn't want to . . . start the honeymoon while all this was hanging over their heads, and Carol said that really she didn't want to either. They sat in their hotel room and talked things over, and Carol said that at least they did *have* each other to chew things over with, and that what they were really facing was the first crisis of their married life. If they could face up to all the others as calmly, things wouldn't work out too badly, would they?

The trouble was, thought David, that facing up to a marriage crisis was one thing, and that could be done calmly and with dignity: but facing up to Joshua Swayne was quite another matter. The mere thought of Joshua made him panic, as facing up to the farm workers had made him sweat in the first weeks of running the Estates after his father's death. It was the thought of him and Carol . . . Well, least said, soonest mended, but somehow David couldn't manage to put that thought out of his head. And it made him the very reverse of calm.

They weren't going to be imprisoned in their room, that was for sure. About three o'clock they went out for a walk, and they probably would have enjoyed it if they hadn't constantly been glancing nervously around to see if they were being shadowed. The island was beautiful, with sloping, fertile pastures, and with cliffs stretching dazzlingly up skywards. Luckily they were young and fit, and David in particular was used to climbing. But as they approached their hotel, the inevitable happened. Joshua was suddenly to be found, insinuating himself beside them.

"Don't you agree it's a beautiful island?" he said. "I thought

I'd let you enjoy it on your own. Went down to Nimos, didn't you? And then up the hill to the coastguard station, then down the cliff path and back here?"

So he had been following them the whole time. David was livid. He drew Carol aside.

"You go ahead, darling," he said. "I'm going to deal with this louse once and for all."

It did not occur to David, in sending Carol on ahead, that really she had a lot more experience in dealing with that louse than he had. Probably even if it had occurred to him he would not have let her do the dealing.

"Now let's get this straight," he said, turning to the imperturbably smiling and disgracefully tanned Joshua. "This has got to stop."

"Spoiling your honeymoon, is it?" asked Joshua.

There seemed nothing for it but to admit it.

"Yes."

Joshua shook his head.

"That's tough. Carol being such a fun girl, and all. She gets whingy when things don't go as she wants them to. Have you found that out yet?"

"She does not get whingy. She is the sweetest girl on God's earth, and you're making her life a misery."

"Now that I would hate to do. If only for old times' sake I'd like her to be happy. Just for her, David—just for her—I might be willing to come to an accommodation."

David was bewildered. Was he offering to seek alternative lodgings?

"I don't get you."

"I might, out of consideration for her, be open to an offer."

David was outraged.

"Do you mean you would accept money to go away?"

Joshua shrugged, still smiling.

"Market forces rule. I'm sure you've always believed that. The plain market fact is that you have money, and I want money."

"You cad! You unadulterated bounder!"

"In addition, the service I can perform for that money is the service you want above all things: I can go away."

"This is unbelievable!"

"You'd better believe it, boyo! I tell you what: you go back to your room and think it over. I can see it's a new idea for you. Never too quick to take in new ideas, are you, David? Then when you've thought it over, talked it through with Carol, you can come up with a sum, and we can start negotiations. How about half past six, up near the coastguard station? There we'll be away from anyone English who might overhear. We wouldn't want either of us to be embarrassed, would we?"

David was, as Joshua implied, not the quickest thinker in the world. He thought over the proposal, and he discussed it with Carol, but after all that he still found the idea utterly distasteful. The trouble was he couldn't think of any alternative to going along with it.

"I think we ought to agree," he said finally. "No—not *ought* to agree: it's a disgusting suggestion. But I think we simply have to."

"I think we have to too," said Carol. "If we don't, then the honeymoon is ruined, and that would be a terrible start to our marriage. And after all, it is only money. It's not nice to be swindled, that's for sure, but on the other hand I don't think we should make money some kind of god. We've got enough of it, heaven knows. . . ."

So six-fifteen saw David toiling up the hill again, once

more leaving Carol out of things, in that old-fashioned, gentlemanly way he had. Carol had not been keen, in any case, to witness a transaction which might almost seem to an outsider to be a sale or auction of herself. David agreed with Carol that they should not make a god of money, but he determined not to offer at the start anything like the sum that he might be prepared to fork out after negotiation.

His heart leapt with justified rage when he saw the figure of Joshua Swayne, on the top of the cliff, silhouetted against the setting sun. He was standing there, rather dejected-looking, and David wondered whether he was perhaps feeling in his heart the jerk his conduct was proving him to be.

"Well," said David, a bit puffed, when he drew near to Joshua. "I've thought it over."

"Yes?" said Joshua, low. David modified his voice too.

"I think we might say three hundred pounds."

"What?" shouted Joshua, suddenly raising his voice, and looking fiercely at David.

"I think we might say four hundred pounds," yelled David in return.

"You swine!" shouted Joshua, in a voice that seemed to carry all over the island. "You absolute cad. My God, you're trying to *buy* me. You think I'm here to screw money out of you! I'm not going to stand for this!"

David did not sense the first blow coming. This was not at all what he had come prepared for. When Joshua engaged him in a close wrestling grip he was too breathless to put up more than a token resistance, and when further blows rained down on him, and they moved closer and closer to the cliff's edge, he could no more avoid the fate he saw coming than can a man in the maelstrom. As he was thrown, head first, over the cliff, he knew his end was a second away, and yet he still did not understand. His overmastering emotion as he fell was bewilderment.

☒

It had all worked out very nicely indeed, Carol considered, as she flew home, dressed in deep black (the Greeks were very good at black, they wore so much of it). She was accompanied by the coffin, but she thought very little about it. That part of her life was over and done with.

The coastguards, whom Joshua had so cleverly ascertained spoke English, testified to the offer of money, and the sense of outrage felt by the accused. The Greek police, being natural romantics and admirers of Milord Byron, had felt considerable sympathy for the young man (did he not resemble in many ways the familiar features of the liberating English Milord?) who had suffered so much at being rejected by the woman he loved, and who was only making a desperate attempt at the very last moment to win her back. To be offered money to go away, this was the ultimate insult to his tender heart. The Greeks, in any case, take a very lenient view of *crimes passionnels*. That, of course, was why she had maneuvered David into choosing Greece. Carol had been assured by the Greek lawyer she had retained for herself (though she had been very cunning about not seeming to ask for any reason other than indignation and pity for the fate of her husband) that Joshua Swayne was unlikely to serve more than five years. ("Alas, madam, but that is how we regard these things in this country!")

Five years! It seemed a lifetime. But her heart swelled with pride as she thought what Joshua was willing to suffer, for her, and for the money. For money there would be, now, in abundance. She did not expect to be well received by David's mother, or his sister, but really there was nothing whatsoever that they could do. From now on she was effective head of Lloyd-Johnson Agricultural Estates. She had always fancied herself running a big business enterprise. When Joshua got out, either they would marry in North Wales and outface the talk or she would sell up and they would branch out into something more glamorous than large-scale farming. The world was all before them.

Joshua was worth waiting for. That she knew for certain. It was very unlikely that she would meet anybody in the next five years who would force her to break her compact with Joshua. She was quite certain she would keep faith with him. Almost a hundred percent certain. It was more than probable that she would.

And if she didn't, of course, there was nothing whatsoever that *he* could do either.

CALLED TO JUDGMENT

When the signal came that the court was ready to begin his trial, the warder to whom the prisoner was handcuffed folded the *Daily Mirror* that he had been reading and stood up. They had exchanged few words in the two hours they had sat there, though the warder did not seem by nature a taciturn individual. As they began down the long, dim corridor toward the dock, he made no concessions to the fact that the prisoner was less used than he was to walking in tandem. He strode ahead, and his yokemate had to try to find the right rhythm to walk easily beside him. When they came to steps leading to a guarded, open door, the warder pushed him ahead and, as the door shut behind them, bent to unlock the handcuffs. All this was done with as little acknowledgment as possible of the prisoner's existence.

It was lighter in the courtroom, and the man blinked to accustom himself to the new brightness. At first he was conscious only of the droning voice of one of the counsels making a procedural point. Then, as he began to look around him, he became aware that the public gallery was full, that some of the people there were straining forward to get a good look at him: a little, birdlike man with no shoulders or chin; a woman in a hat like a squashed rabbit, with a hungry, malevolent expression. He should have expected it, but in fact he had hardly thought about the trial at all, and had been brought to court by a back entrance to avoid the crowds that had gathered. He squared his shoulders, sat up straight, and stared back at the gallery. He was not going to act guilty, ashamed, self-conscious—not he.

Counsel had finished making his point and sat down. That was the prosecuting counsel. His own silk he recognized, having talked to him, though only once. A smooth, near-handsome man with his way to make in his profession and a determination to make it. Eyes would be on him at this trial, and he would be eager to impress. The judge too was young for a judge—a recent appointment by a Lord Chancellor anxious to dispel the public's notion that the bench consisted of elderly fuddy-duddies quite unacquainted with the modern world.

The judge's head was down when the prisoner looked in his direction. He was making a lengthy note on the points raised by the prosecuting counsel. All the prisoner could see was the top of his wig. Then he finished his notes, pushed away the paper, and raised his head, to look directly into the prisoner's eyes.

The name Denzil Charlton had featured prominently in the Macmillan household when Roderick was growing up.

"Let's have you neat and tidy," his mother would say as she adjusted his tie and put his cap on straight. "We can't have Denzil Charlton's mummy looking down her nose, can we?"

Denzil Charlton's mummy loomed large in Roderick's mother's demonology, but Denzil himself had made little or no impression on Roderick. He wasn't in his form, for a start, and he certainly wasn't one of his friends. Roderick's main memory was of Mrs. Charlton waiting for her son at the school gates. She was a figure (as he would put it now) of overpowering respectability—or, as his mother explained at the time, "very proper." Little Denzil was brought to school with his shoes gleaming, his tie squarely in the center of his neck, not a hair out of place, and he was expected to be in the same state when he was fetched home in the afternoon. Even at a small private school in a Home Counties town this was thought to be excessive. Other mothers who collected their sons noted Mrs. Charlton's expression of disapproval at any sign of dirt or untidiness on their sons, or even if they ran to greet their mothers when they came out of the gate. "I hate to think what her house is like," said one mother, daring to voice the general feeling. Another even dared to quote *Under Milk Wood*—"And before you let the sun in, mind it wipes its shoes"—though the other mothers didn't quite see the joke. The mother who said: "Poor little mite—he can hardly dare breathe," about summed up the general feeling.

But then one summer the Charltons moved away, and Denzil Charlton's mummy remained only for a few more months as a bogey figure in the Macmillan home.

"Can't have you with jam on your chin, in case Mrs. Charlton decides to come back," Roderick's mother said. But like all bogey figures, Mrs. Charlton had had her day, and soon her absence meant that she was forgotten entirely.

Denzil Charlton had no memories of Roddy Macmillan going back to school days. All his own early school memories, in fact, were centered on the respectable London school in the respectable London suburb to which his parents moved when he was seven, then later the minor public school to which he was sent when he was thirteen. He had asked to go to boarding school, and while he was at Repton he always participated in foreign trips and adventure schools during the vacations. His parents put no obstacles in his way. He had flourished at Repton, though the master who had kept the closest eye on him uttered the stiff judgment that he was "a bit wild." It was a verdict which his fellow pupils, particularly those who had been on the foreign trips, would have agreed with.

Denzil's first memory of Roddy concerned a certain party in London. It was the day after the last exam of Finals, and he had no memory of how the party had been arranged, except that most of the men were rowing men from various colleges, so presumably it had been a rowing man who had organized it and asked his friends along. The evening had begun with boisterous drinks at a London flat—it was a case of parents who were abroad—and then the twenty-odd hearty young men had gone to a nightclub somewhere near St. Martin's Lane.

The Casablanca was used to rowdies, but when the manager saw the size of the party he rang round for supplementary bouncers. For the first couple of hours the young men up from Oxford were in high good humor, but the manager knew that anything or nothing would change their mood. It was in fact easy to pinpoint the time when things turned nasty. It was during the floor show, when one of the solo dancers was judged to be not up to par—to be, in fact, "over the hill," as one of the young men ungallantly pointed out in a loud voice. The manager focused his attention on him.

Denzil Charlton was sitting, quite by chance, next to Roddy Macmillan, their chairs turned around from their table to watch the show. They had not exchanged a word thus far into the evening, but soon after he had given his opinion of the dancer Denzil turned to his neighbor.

"I'm Denzil Charlton," he said, putting out his hand.

"I'm Roddy Macmillan."

Was it something in the quieter man that seemed to challenge Charlton? Did he mistake an expression in his eye—a groping recognition that he knew the name, perhaps—for something else? Whatever it was, it seemed to act as some sort of challenge. Denzil got louder and louder. "Crap!" he shouted at the dancer, then something nastier at the next act. "Tell her she's shit-awful," he encouraged Roddy, and Roddy voiced a loud, drunken expression of opprobrium. Then they started breaking up bread rolls and throwing them. That was when the heavies moved in. Denzil tried to get a general fight going, but the others were mostly enjoying themselves. The bouncers targeted well. Three of the ringleaders were seized and frog-marched out, down dim corridors, then out of a back entrance and into a dingy, rubbish-strewn back alley. One of them immediately passed out in a doorway. That left Denzil and Roddy looking at each other.

"Christ, I need a woman," said Denzil.

Roddy Macmillan's memories of that night really began at that point. They remained so vivid partly because of the man, partly because of what subsequently happened and was said. His sexual experience thus far had consisted of an encounter with a maid at his grandparents' home (guilty and unsatisfactory) and more pleasurable sessions with girls he had met while walking in the Lake District, on Skye, and in the Loire Valley. He had never been with a prostitute—had regarded them, when accosted in London, with something like fear. Now he felt a firm hand on his shoulder that propelled him in the direction of Leicester Square. Down an arcade lined with expensive antiquarian bookshops he threw up. At least that cleared his head and made him feel better. Once Leicester Square had been circumnavigated they plunged into Soho.

Denzil certainly knew what he was doing.

"We'll go to Ma Hartley's," he said. "Better choice. Ma Cook's is nearer, but she's got some rotten bits of flesh, and sometimes you have to take what you can get. Don't tangle with Ma Hartley. She's as tough as old boots."

Ma Hartley didn't seem overpleased to see Denzil. "Oh, it's you again, is it?" she said. She seemed somewhat mollified when she saw he'd brought a friend along, but she remained standing in the doorway until the details of the deal had been settled. She offered Denzil a choice of Bridget, Gloria, and Vi, and he chose Vi, recommending Roddy to take Bridget. Ma shouted "Vi and Bridget" into the back, took their money, and then said: "First floor, room on your left" to Denzil, and "Second floor, straight ahead" to Roddy. Roddy found Bridget to belie her convent name by being an efficient and no-nonsense performer. He himself felt intimidated by the thought of all his predecessors, and his proceedings resembled nothing so much as that first time with his grandparents' maid. He stayed on his back talking for five minutes afterward, but he found the woman as uninteresting as thousands had before him. Soon he put himself to rights and staggered downstairs.

He stopped on the corner of Dean Street to light himself a cigarette. Behind him he heard a door shut. It was Denzil Charlton. When he came up he was oddly excited.

"Thought I heard you," he said, trying to keep his voice matter-of-fact. "Not a bad lay, is she?"

"Not bad," said Roddy, equally casual. "I've had better." They began to walk toward Piccadilly.

"Give her a good poke, did you?" Denzil asked with a leer. "Rod by name, Rod by nature."

"I'm not mad about prostitutes," said Roddy, world-weary. "I prefer a partner who shows some interest."

"I love whores." This came out with a break in the voice. Roddy threw a quick look at him and did not like what he saw. "They excite me," Charlton went on. "Their *awfulness* excites me. Their horrible 'I'll lie here while you do whatever you want to with me' sort of attitude. If they can be said to have such a thing as an attitude. They're just disgusting human beings. The dregs. The pits. That's what excites me. They oughtn't to be allowed to go on existing. They're hardly part of the human race at all."

Roddy's instinct was to try to cool it.

"To each his own choice of vocation," he said lightly. Denzil Charlton's face twisted.

"They don't choose it. They're fit for nothing else, capable of nothing else. Those whores are down there in the sewer because it's their natural habitat."

"I'd have thought the best thing was not to go within a mile of them if you felt like that."

"Do you think so?" Denzil felt in his pocket. "I keep a knife. Sometimes when we're . . . at it, I get the idea that when we're done—when I'm done, because the whore is just done *to*—I'll take the knife and I'll plunge it in when she's lying there, like a lump of dough, plunge it into her and do a nice little surgical job, just like Jack the Ripper used to do." They were passing a streetlight, and the knife glinted dangerously in his young hand. It was a stubby, substantial knife, not something for a lethal slide through the ribs into the heart, but seemingly made for cruder work entirely. "Feel it. Feel how sharp and tough it is." Roddy shook his head quickly and looked away. "Eviscerate—that's a lovely word, isn't it? Much nicer than disembowel—though perhaps that is closer to the nature of the operation. You know, I understand him, old Jack. I know how he felt, what he wanted to do. He was performing an act of public hygiene."

They plunged down into the underground.

"I'm for the Bakerloo Line," said Roddy, as Denzil Charlton made for the Piccadilly Line. He strode away, telling himself that he had never been happier at parting from anybody. Was the man a psychopath or a tease? If he was the latter he had never failed so entirely to pick up any signs of humor or fun.

But when he sat in his carriage and began analyzing his feelings in the cool, detached way that he had, he started to wonder if the emotion he had felt at the young man's revelation of his instinctive urges was not nausea and disgust, as he had thought at first, but excitement.

It was eight years before the two men met again. They both lived in London now, but they moved in very different circles, one in banking, the other in law. It was at a charity dinner in Wimbledon, one overheavy with male eaters, that Roderick Macmillan, about to sit down, found he had men to the right and left of him—a situation he disliked. To his right was a very dull local councillor whom he had been bored by at previous dinners and receptions. Looking down at the tag to his left he saw in pseudo-Gothic script the name Denzil Charlton.

He looked up sharply as the man slipped into his place. A glance of mutual recognition passed between them.

"Long time, as they say, no see," said Charlton easily.

"Yes. . . . Sad shortage of ladies here tonight," said Roderick, as his social contribution.

"Does that worry you?" asked Charlton, with the suspicion of a sneer. "Have you brought your own lady along?"

"No," admitted Roderick, wishing he'd avoided the topic of women entirely. "My wife should have come but our little girl has teething problems, and she preferred to stay at home."

"Tough."

"Perhaps not so tough," said Roderick, looking round the dull assembly. They both laughed. "And you?"

"No lady. No wife, and no other kind of lady."

They set to quietly on the soup, which was unidentifiable.

"Wife, little girl, obviously prosperous—you're climbing up the greasy pole gracefully I presume?" asked Denzil, always with that suspicion of a sneer.

"Moderately gracefully. So much is changing in the legal world that the goalposts are shifting the whole time."

"Same thing in banking. Technology keeps us all on our toes. And there's always the fear that out there some computer whiz kid is lurking who is two or three steps ahead of us in the technology game."

"Frightening. That's not something we have to worry about in the legal profession."

"No. . . . But there's one way in which both professions have changed together."

"What's that?"

"We're no longer respectable in the way we used to be. No one trusts the professions as they once did. Bankers used to be super-buttoned-up, and so did lawyers. The breath of scandal or malpractice and no one wanted to know them. Now . . ."

Roderick nodded thoughtfully.

"Now. . . . Yes, you're right. Bankers and solicitors are disappearing with the loot all the time, or being caught with their hands in their clients' funds."

"Not to mention their *private* behavior," said Denzil Charlton. Roderick Macmillan ate on in silence. Denzil smiled at his caution with a relish he could not bestow on the food.

"You know, I think it's a pity, in a way," he went on. "That the old taboos are falling by the wayside, I mean. They made for such a piquant contrast, and gave such a delicious sense of danger to private vices. The Victorians had it right after all. Whatever happened to reticence? To discretion? Soon we'll have lawyers pleading in court in blond wigs and miniskirts and special gay bankers to advise minorities on their financial problems. Takes all the zest away from vice."

"I should have thought there were some vices that still had the zest of danger attached to them," said Roddy, a tiny choke in his voice. Denzil laughed heartily.

"Ah, you're referring to my secret fantasies about whores. Maybe, maybe. Though this is the eighties, old son. You can talk these days about people who aren't worth the airspace they take up, you can talk about a class that shouldn't be allowed to breed. That's another old taboo that has gone. . . . Though I admit that some other aspects of my fantasy are best left unspoken even now."

"There was a case . . . last year . . . of a prostitute in Swansea who was . . . cut about . . . in the way you . . ."

"Really?" Denzil came back, imperturbably cheerful. "Never been to Swansea. Don't fancy it. I imagine the whores as being dark, gnomelike creatures with impenetrable accents, hangovers from the Celtic hegemony. Am I right? But I say, it proves one thing, doesn't it?"

"What?"

"There's others share my instincts about what should be done with these scrubbers. But perhaps you know that already. Eh, Roddy? Did you know that already? Do you feel it yourself?"

Roddy was actually glad that, at the head of the table, a local nonentity had got up to speak.

※

In the darkness he sat on the bed trying not to think of the thing beside him. The thing he had made—the hideous, bloody thing. And trying not to think, too, of the excitement he had felt as he did it. It was not to be thought of, it had to be put behind him. The important thing was now to be practical. The only thing that mattered was getting away.

But not just getting away—getting back into his hotel room as well. The dingy light in this dismal whorehouse would help. And people didn't look at you closely in brothels. Clients didn't like it, nor the girls particularly: it made the whole thing look too much like a slave auction. But once he got back to the hotel? It was not a hotel he had ever stayed at before—one of the government's economy measures. It was now after midnight. Would it have subdued lighting in the foyer and the corridors? Some did, some didn't.

There was a dirty little basin in the corner. Soap but no flannel. *Cold* water—only cold water, dammit. He reached into his pocket and pulled out an immaculate white handkerchief. Not immaculate for long. Carefully, with painstaking thoroughness, he washed his hands, and then his face and neck, then put the reddened square of cotton back into his pocket. Averting his eyes from the bed, he took his tie and jacket from the hook on the door and put them on. He stood by the door, listening. In such a place there were always noises. Noises from the business that was being paid for. Noises of people coming, people going. He heard footsteps, then the front door slamming. Then silence.

Now.

He opened the door, slipped through it, then shut it on the hideous spectacle on the bed. Then he walked as casually as he could down the stairs, taking care on the threadbare carpet, then along the dim hallway and out into the street. Once there he turned in the direction of the main road.

That was better lit. In fact, under a bright streetlight a man was pausing to light a cigarette. A man whose shape, form, carriage he recognized. A man whom he had once been with in similar circumstances in an alleyway off Dean Street.

But this time there was to be no meeting. He held back in the darkness until the figure turned to his right, then walked slowly to the main road and turned off to the left.

The routine preliminaries to the trial were drawing to a close. Mr. Justice Macmillan had paid them what attention he could, occasionally adding to his notes. His gaze mostly went from his notes to counsel and then back again. The atmosphere in the courtroom was as electric as he had ever known it. The handsome arrogance of the accused, the vicious nature of the crime he was accused of, ensured that. Mr. Justice Macmillan was particularly conscious of the gimlet eyes of a lady with a squashed fur hat, and the twisted leer of a man whose body was like a chicken's carcass. Both of them seemed to him like malevolent gods, as their eyes went hungrily from accused to judge and back to accused. They have already decided that he is guilty, thought the judge. Back and forth the eyes went, from guilty to innocent, innocent to guilty. But only one man in the courtroom knew, really *knew*, which was which.

More Final Than Divorce

*G*erry Porter had no desire to murder his wife. He would much have preferred simply to trade her in for a new model. But Gerry was a businessman, and he knew how to do his sums. He totted up the value of his butchery business, of their house and two cars, of the time-share villa in Spain. He knew it was no longer a question simply of paying her a pittance as alimony—that the judge would award his wife a substantial proportion of the marital estate. Every way he looked at it it was impossible for him to keep his business, a roof over his head and a new wife. He sighed. It would have to be something more final than divorce. It would have to be murder. Personally, he told himself, he blamed these feminists. If it hadn't been for these new divorce laws Sandra would be alive today.

Well, actually Sandra *was* alive today. That was, of course, the problem. He didn't think Sandra had any suspicions about the newer model, but the moment she did she'd tell her friends, and therein would lie the danger. For Gerry was determined that the police should not hear about the newer model, because he had no intention that Sandra's death should be treated as a case of murder. Everyone knew who the first suspect was when a wife or husband was murdered. No, Sandra was not going to be murdered. Sandra was going to have an accident. Or commit suicide.

Gerry went about it in a methodical way. There were always plenty of newspapers around in his butcher's shop as wrapping, and between customers he studied them avidly.

Plenty of people did die by accident, and the inquests on them were reported in the local rag. Gerry began classifying them in his mind into road accidents, domestic accidents and accidents at work. The last category was out, since Sandra did not go to work. The first category was large, and encompassed many different kinds of death in or under motor vehicles. Gerry did notice how many people seemed to die on holiday abroad, and he toyed with the idea of getting some Spaniard to run into her or run her down on some particularly dangerous stretch of Iberian road. But the thought of being in the power of some greasy wop (Gerry was neither a liberal nor a tolerant thinker) made him go off the idea. And the more he read about the advances in forensic science, the less inclined he felt to tamper with his wife's car.

But the more he thought about it, the same objection seemed to apply to domestic accidents. People did electrocute themselves; some even, apparently (God, what ignorant bastards people were!), perched electric fires on the ends of their baths. But the Porters had central heating, and Gerry doubted his ability to render their high-speed kettle lethal in a way that would fool Forensics.

Gerry was sent off on to another tack entirely one evening when he passed the living room while his wife was having coffee with a friend, and heard her say:

"Oh God, the Change! There's times I've wondered whether I'll ever get through it."

Gerry was a heavy man, with heavy footsteps, and he could not stop to hear any more. Sandra in fact went on to say that luckily she now seemed to be over the worst. Gerry had gone on to the front door, and out to the garage, and a little idea was jigging around in his mind. Gone were thoughts of accidents with car exhaust fumes, of pushing Sandra under an underground train. Suicide while the balance of her mind was disturbed. Or, to be more precise, the balance of her body.

With no plan as yet firmly formulated, he nevertheless began laying the ground next evening in the pub.

"You're very thoughtful, Gerry," said Sam Eagleton to him as he sat over his second pint. And indeed he was. It was quite a strain. Because Gerry was usually the life and soul of the Cock and Pheasant, with a steady stream of salacious, off-color or racist jokes.

"Aye. It's the wife. She's a bit under the weather. . . ." After a pause, occupied with a gaze into the brown depths of his beer mug, he added: "It's the Change. It's a rotten thing to have to go through. It does things to a woman. We can count ourselves lucky we don't have anything like it."

It was a most un-Gerry-like topic of conversation. Sam Eagleton thought it a bit off to mention it at all, and not good form, as it was understood at the Cock and Pheasant. He said: "Aye, it's a bad business," and changed the subject.

In the Cock and Pheasant and other places that Gerry Porter frequented, they got used to the topic of the Change over the next few weeks. It was supplemented by other causes of worry and distress to Sandra, for Gerry had decided that her suicide would be the result of a cumulative burden of miseries, of myriad worries that finally became too much to bear.

"The wife's mother is in a bad way," he would say. "Senile. It's a terrible burden on Sandra."

Gerry's mother-in-law was in a Home, and he had in the past made ribald jokes about her increasingly erratic behavior. Now, apparently, all he could see was the distress that it must cause his wife.

"Gerry's gone all serious on us," said his friend Paul Tutin when he had gone out one evening, still long-faced. The

Cock and Pheasant was not bright enough to be suspicious, but it was puzzled.

There were other problems and vicissitudes in the Porter household that were tediously canvassed. Sandra's attempts to get O Level English, one of the things she studied at one of her many evening classes, had hitherto been the subject of innumerable sexist jokes about the thickness of women. Now all they heard was what a terrible grief it was to her. "But she shouldn't be trying to get it now," he would say. "Not while she's going through the Change." The Porters had no children to cause them worry, but nephews and nieces were press-ganged into service, and a brother of Sandra who was serving a jail sentence was represented as an agonizing worry. But in the end it all came back to the Change.

"It does something to some women," Gerry would say. "You've no idea. Sometimes I wonder if it's the same woman I married. She says that every morning she dreads waking up."

One afternoon, while she was shopping in Doncaster, Sandra dropped into the Cherry Tree Tea Shop, and was glad to see two of her old friends sitting in the window. They waved her over to their table.

"Hello, Sandra, how *are* you?" Mary Eagleton hailed.

"Fine," said Sandra, sitting down. "Just fine."

"Oh, good. I *am* glad. Gerry was telling Sam the other night that the good old menopause was getting you down."

"A lot Gerry knows about it."

"When are you taking your O Level again?" asked Mary over the cream cakes.

"Next week!" said Sandra, roaring with laughter. "And I haven't opened a book since I failed last time. I bet the examiners are sharpening their pencils and licking their lips over the thought of giving me bottom grades."

"How's your mother?" asked Brenda Tutin.

"Great! Completely gaga. Doesn't even know me when I go in, so I've stopped going. It's a great relief."

"Gerry says you're very upset about it," said Brenda.

Sandra raised her eyebrows.

"What *exactly* has Gerry been saying?" she asked.

Things went on pretty much as normal in the next few weeks. Sandra took up yet another evening class—cake decorating, of all things—and so they saw very little of each other, except at breakfast. Gerry insisted on the full menu with trimmings at breakfast time—porridge, egg and bacon with sausage and tomato, two or three slices of toast and marmalade. He said it set him up for the day. Sandra, who had been to diet classes and keep-fit classes, found cooking it rather nauseating, but she didn't have to watch him eat it, because he propped up his *Sun* newspaper against the coffeepot and devoured its edifying contents along with the bacon and sausage.

He was back from the pub (or from the newer model) more often in the evenings now when she got back from her classes. He was even rather considerate, something he had not been for many years, in fact not since the first week of their honeymoon. When she flopped down in the armchair ("Everything seems to tire her now," he said in the pub) he offered her a vodka and tonic, and was even prepared to make her a mug of Ovaltine. Sometimes she accepted, sometimes she did not. It was certainly pleasant to have him actually doing something for her in the kitchen. ("She's been desperate for sleep," Gerry planned to tell the police. "She's been trying everything.")

The crunch came nearly six months after Gerry had first made his decision. Sandra got back from evening classes and was ex*haus*ted, she said.

"Vodka and tonic, darling?" Gerry asked.

"That *would* be nice, Smoochie," she said, using a pet name they had almost abandoned.

When he brought it over Sandra noticed that he was not smelling of beer. She snuggled up on the sofa in front of the roaring gas fire.

"This is the life!" she said.

Gerry was watching her as she tasted her drink, though ostensibly he was at the sideboard, getting one for himself. She gave no sign that it tasted any different, and he breathed out. She swung her feet up on to the sofa, and took another sip or two of the vodka and tonic.

"Funny," she said. "I feel famished."

"Let me get you something."

"Would you, Smoochie? Just a few biscuits, and a bit of cheese."

When he got back the vodka and tonic was half drunk. Sandra ate the biscuits and cheese ravenously.

"I don't know why cake decorating should be so *grueling*," she said, taking a good swig at her drink. "I could almost settle down to sleep here in front of the fire."

"Why don't you?" Gerry said, sitting down by the head of the sofa and running his fingers through her hair. Sandra downed the rest of her drink.

"Lovely not to have the television on," she said, her voice seeming to come from far away. Her head dropped on to the arm of the sofa, her eyes closed. Soon Gerry heard gentle snores.

He jumped up and looked at his watch. It was just after ten. He could aim at the 10:45 or the 10:55. Both were expresses, and both were usually on time. He put in his pocket a little bottle of prepared vodka and sleeping draft.

("She had it with her drink. I thought she wanted to sleep; I didn't realize she wanted it to deaden the pain," he would tell the police.) He intended to force it down her throat if she should show signs of waking up. Then he went out into the drive and opened both doors of his wife's little Fiat (his own Range Rover always had the garage). Then he went back into the sitting room, took his wife gently in his arms and carried her through the front door and out to the car. He laid her gently in the front passenger seat, and got in beside her.

The drive to the bridge was uneventful, though Gerry was bathed in sweat by the end of it. They met no more than three or four cars going in the other direction. After only ten minutes they turned into the narrow road, scarcely more than a track, which led to the railway bridge. His heart banged with relief as he parked Sandra's car under a clump of trees.

He looked at his watch. Ten minutes to go before the 10:45 went by, if it was on time. He looked at his wife. She was breathing deeply, her head lolling to one side. The Sovipol he had got from the doctor ("*She* can't sleep, Doctor, and that means *I* don't sleep, and it's affecting the business") was working like a dream. He got out of the car, leaned back in, and with a butcher's strength he lifted Sandra across into the driver's seat.

He wiped the steering wheel, then put her fingers on it in two or three different positions. Then he let them fall, and pressed the little bottle of vodka and Sovipol into them. ("I was already in bed," he would tell the police. "I'd had a hard day. I was knackered. I did hear her driving off, but I thought she must have left something behind at her class. She's been getting very forgetful since the Change started. . . .")

Time to get her on to the bridge. It was an old one, dating from the time when this neglected track was an important road. He took her in his arms and carried her—almost tenderly—the hundred yards there. No sound of a train yet. He laid her in a sitting position by the bridge and then straightened. God, he could do with a fag. But would that be wise? No—there in the distance was the regular hum of the diesel: the Intercity 125 from King's Cross to Leeds. He waited a moment. It wouldn't be here for a minute or two yet. Thank God he hadn't needed to force the contents of the bottle down her. As it was, his nerves were stretched beyond bearing by tension. He wanted to wet himself. Then, as the noise of the train grew nearer, he stretched down to the comatose figure by the bridge. He put his hands under the body.

And immediately he felt an open palm smash suddenly into his face. In a moment it was he who was on his back across the parapet of the bridge. Suddenly it was his wife who had strong hands on his shoulders, his wife who was pushing, pushing. Dimly he heard her voice.

"They were karate classes, Smoochie. Karate classes."

Then she dropped him into the path of the oncoming express.

The police were by and large extremely sympathetic. It was child's play to them to unravel the details of Gerry's plan. They talked to his friends and heard about his change of character in his pub sessions, the conversations that had prepared the way. They found his dolly bird in a little flat in central Doncaster (though she said she would never have married him, not in a million years). They found the railway timetables in his study, analyzed the earth in the pot plant into which Sandra Porter had poured most of her drink. ("It tasted so off. I thought he'd given me gin by mistake, which I hate, and I didn't want to offend him.") They talked to the neighbor who had passed them on the road and seen that it was Gerry driving, talked to the poacher who had seen Gerry park the car and seen him press Sandra's hands to the steering wheel. *Those* prints wouldn't have deceived a rookie constable that they were those of a woman actually driving a car. No, Gerry Porter would never have got away with it, even if he had succeeded in killing his wife.

Sandra was quite affecting. She had drunk about a quarter of her drink, she said, but had filled the glass up with tonic water so he shouldn't know. ("He could be awfully touchy," she said.) What she had drunk had sent her soundly to sleep. When she began to awaken she was in the car, in the driving seat, and her husband was pressing her hands to the steering wheel. She was confused and terrified. How had she got there? What was going on? She had feigned sleep until she had heard the train, her husband had lifted her up, and then she—terrified— had used the techniques she had learnt at self-defense classes. ("The police are always recommending that we do them, and with the number of ghastly rapes we've had around here . . .")

Only Inspector Potter of the South Yorkshire CID had doubts.

"Why weren't there more signs of struggle?" he asked. "Why did she make no attempt to immobilize him rather than kill him? Why did she take up karate classes, midterm, after he'd started laying the ground in his pubs? Why did she take such care, driving to the Doncaster police station, not to disturb the fake prints?"

"She *had* to kill him," said his superintendent. "Otherwise he'd have been stalking her through the woods. She was practically out of her mind."

"Yet she was careful not to disturb those prints. . . . Oh, I grant you there's no point in nagging away at it. It's an academic exercise. We'd never secure a conviction, not even for manslaughter. Never in a million years."

But the doubts remained in his mind. He noticed that a few days after the inquest and funeral, Porter's Family Butchery was open again for business. He noted that Sandra ran it very efficiently, with the help of a stalwart chap, fifteen years her junior, whom he heard she had met at karate class. When, a year after Gerry's death, he saw in the paper that she had married him, he showed the announcement to the superintendent.

"We'd never have got a conviction," he repeated. "But she did it very nicely, didn't she? Got her freedom, her boyfriend *and* the whole of the property. Beats a divorce settlement anytime! He handed himself to her on a plate, did Gerry Porter. On a ruddy plate!"